LEFT-HANDED SHORTSTOP

Rat Teeth tried to steal second.

GI

$\mathcal{L}$EFT-HANDED SHORTSTOP

PATRICIA REILLY GIFF

Illustrated by Leslie Morrill

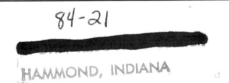
Delacorte Press/ New York

Published by
Delacorte Press
1 Dag Hammarskjold Plaza
New York, New York 10017

Manufactured in the United States of America
Second Printing—1981

Designed by Oksana Kushnir

LIBRARY OF CONGRESS CATALOGING IN PUBLICATION DATA
Giff, Patricia Reilly.
Left-handed shortstop.

SUMMARY: When his classmates brag that Walter is their star
shortstop, Walter makes a cast for his left arm so the kids won't
see what a terrible player he really is.
[1. Baseball—Fiction]   I. Morrill, Leslie H.   II. Title.
PZ7.G3626Le   [Fic]   80-65835
ISBN 0-440-04553-3
ISBN 0-440-04554-1   lib. bdg.

FOR SHORTSTOPS
RIGHT-HANDED AND LEFT
AND FOR SOME SPECIAL BALL PLAYERS—
JIM, JIMMY, AND BILLY GIFF
AND FREDDIE MOELLER

I should like to thank
Nancy Blumenberg, Alethea Jackson, Dennis Lawlor,
and Keith Romano for their help.

P. R. G.

1

Walter Moles was late, as usual. It didn't seem to make any difference that he lived right on the same block as the Ogden Street School. Every day he was the last one in.

Walter jumped off the three brick steps in front of his house, circled around the driveway into his yard, and climbed the Cyclone fence into the alley between his house and the school. He and his friend Casey Valentine called the alley the Secret Passageway because no one else ever used it. It was just a narrow space full of weeds and the junk that blew in from the schoolyard.

Walter stood in the alley for several seconds checking out their latest experiment, a pail of muddy water he and Casey had put there four or five days ago. Now that it was warm, maybe they could get something to grow in it, fish or plants . . . anything.

Since he was going to be an ecologist when he grew up, he figured it was about time he learned all about things springing to life in the water.

He stirred the brown water with a wooden spoon. Yesterday he and Casey had noticed some little stringy things floating around on top. But nothing much seemed to be happening. Maybe in a day or two. . . .

He poked at his eyeglasses and glanced over at the schoolyard. Today wasn't going to be just an ordinary school day. Their teacher, Mrs. Petty, had left on Friday because she had won a trip to India in a crossword puzzle contest. She had told the class there would be a new teacher on Monday. He wondered if she'd be as tough as Mrs. Petty had been.

Walter dropped the spoon behind the pail, wiped his hands on his jacket, and vaulted the fence into the schoolyard. The fourth-grade line was snaking its way through the big gray double doors when he caught it. He spotted J.R. Fiddle and slipped in behind him. J.R. was the skinniest kid in the fourth grade and the longest talker. He had seen about a thousand movies and knew about ten thousand baseball facts and would talk about every one of them all day if he could.

Right now J.R. was leaning over Casey, who was in front of him in the line. He was mumbling to her nonstop. Out of the corner of his eye he spotted Walter behind him and craned his neck around toward the end of the hall to make sure the monitor wasn't look-

2

ing their way. "Hey, Moles," he said in a loud whisper, keeping his eyes on the back of Casey's head. "I was just telling Valentine about something I saw on television. *Lightning in the Valley.* Did you see it?"

Walter opened his mouth to answer, but before he could say a word, J.R. said, "Guns shooting all over the place. Pshu, pshu. Guys getting shot. Agh. Agh." He clutched his throat and staggered up the stairs leading to their classroom. At the top he nudged Casey. "I'll start at the beginning again. Tell old Moles what happened."

Walter pretended to pay attention as they marched down the hall, but he was really thinking about the new teacher and what she'd be like. Besides, he had seen about ten minutes of *Lightning in the Valley.* Worst thing he had seen all year.

Casey ran her tongue over her braces and looked back at Walter. She had seen *Lightning in the Valley* too.

Walter followed along as the line turned into Room 214. He stopped dead when he reached the door. He couldn't believe it. The new teacher sitting at the desk in front of the room was a man. He motioned for the class to come in. "Stand around the side of the room and the back," he said in a booming voice.

He waited until the class filed in. The last three in the line, Walter, J.R., and Casey, ended up along the side of the room, close to the teacher's desk. The man had curly black hair and was so fat his backside spilled over the edges of the chair. "My name is Mr. Dengle," he said finally, "and I'm going to be your teacher for the rest of the year."

3

Walter still couldn't believe it. There had never been a man teacher at the Ogden Street School.

J.R. cupped his hand around his mouth and jerked his head toward Mr. Dengle. "Wow," he whispered to Walter. "That teacher's all beef from the hoof up."

Walter laughed.

Mr. Dengle frowned. "What's your name?"

Walter pointed to himself. "You mean me?" He wiggled his toes nervously in his sneakers. "Walter. Walter Moles."

"Of course I mean you. Don't start anything so early in the morning."

Walter lowered his head and stared at a pink eraser that Albert Fein and Gunther Reed were kicking across the back of the room.

"That goes for the rest of you," Mr. Dengle said.

The door opened and Walter looked up. It was Ellen Marino from the fifth grade. She had a note in her hand. From the way she clumped, Walter guessed she was wearing new shoes. He glanced at her feet. The shoes were tall and chunky.

"Can I give this to my brother, Mitchell?" Ellen asked Mr. Dengle, waving the note in the air.

"May I," said Mr. Dengle. He hesitated for a moment. "All right. If it's important."

Ellen handed the note to Mitchell and clumped out of the room. She was sucking in her cheeks so hard that Walter figured she had blisters already.

Mr. Dengle began to tell everybody about all the wonderful things that were going to happen in Room 214 now that he was their teacher. But Walter wasn't really paying much attention. He looked around at

4

the rest of the class. Nobody else was listening to Mr. Dengle either. They were all watching Mitchell Marino.

As soon as Mitchell had unfolded the note and read it, he folded it up again and passed it to Gunther Reed.

Gunther read it quickly, grinned, then nudged Charlie Eels, who was standing next to him. Charlie held out his hand and took the paper.

"Yes," Mr. Dengle was saying, "we'll take a trip to the City Art Museum. Study some famous—" He broke off. "BRING ME THAT NOTE, YOUNG MAN."

For a moment there was silence. Everyone looked at Charlie. Then Charlie slouched up to the front of the room and gave Mr. Dengle the note. As Charlie went back to his seat, Walter could see that his face was as red as his shirt.

Mr. Dengle read the note. "Well, class. I don't know why the boys didn't share this with the whole class. This is a challenge from some of the fifth graders. They want to meet the fourth-grade boys for a baseball game tomorrow after school."

He put the note on his desk. "Terrific idea. I'd come to watch you but I have an appointment at three o'clock."

The class started to buzz. Walter shifted from one foot to the other. He wished Mr. Dengle would tell them to sit down.

"Same guys as last year," Gunther Reed yelled. "I'm pitcher. Charlie Eels is shortstop."

"Yeah," Albert Fein yelled. "Charlie's the best shortstop in the whole school."

Charlie ducked his head and grinned.

5

Suddenly Mr. Dengle got up from his chair, knocking it over backward. "Just what I like to see. A little competition."

He crouched down, grabbed an imaginary bat, and began to swing it in wide circles. "Yes, sir," he said. "And I expect you to win."

He stopped swinging. "Tell you what," he said. "Just to make things a little more exciting . . ." He paused and thought for a moment. "If you win the game, I'll excuse you from homework on Friday nights for the rest of the year."

The class began to clap. Gunther Reed gave a piercing whistle. Walter clapped his hands over his ears.

Mr. Dengle pounded on his desk for order. When the class was finally quiet, he said, "I have another announcement for you. There's going to be a city-wide science fair next month for fourth and fifth graders. Each class will choose two representatives to make a project and attend the fair."

Mr. Dengle looked around. "I don't know who the class scientists are," he said. "But I'll find out soon."

Walter glanced at Casey. She looked back at him and grinned. They were sure to be picked. He could tell she knew just what he was thinking. They'd have to look through their experiment book, see if they could get something together.

"Now," Mr. Dengle said, "I'm going to let you sit where you want. Just until I find out who the trouble-makers are." He smiled for about half a minute, showing thick, tan teeth. "Go ahead, pick a seat."

The girls raced for the front of the room; the boys dove for the back. Charlie Eels, the class shortstop,

6

slid into a chair. Half the boys scrambled to sit near him. So did a few of the girls. J.R. Fiddle jumped over a desk and landed in back of Charlie.

Walter shook his head and ambled toward a desk at the back of the room. It was the last seat left. He couldn't understand the fuss. Nobody had paid attention to Charlie Eels all year. He had been just another kid. But now it looked as if Charlie was going to be a star.

But he wasn't going to be a star for long. Charlie's father had gotten a new job in Philadelphia and the Eelses were moving in two weeks.

Mr. Dengle banged a book on his desk. "Well, boys and girls. The rest of the year is going to be interesting, I can promise you that." He waved his hand. "But right now we're going to start with some interesting assignments. How many of you would like to write your autobiography?"

Two or three kids raised their hands halfheartedly. Most of the others looked down at their desks or out the window. The only one who really looked happy about writing the story of her life, Walter thought, was Casey Valentine. And that was because Casey wanted to be a writer when she grew up. She was always wasting time writing to her pen pal, Tracy Matson.

"Yes, class," said Mr. Dengle, breaking into Walter's thoughts, "I knew you'd be interested."

J.R. raised his hand. "I think I'll pass."

"Pass?" Mr. Dengle repeated. "Pass? Let's get this straight right from the beginning. When I make a suggestion, it's an order. And right now I'm suggesting

7

you write an autobiography." Mr. Dengle sat down. "And it better be at least a hundred words."

Walter sighed. Mr. Dengle wasn't going to be any better than Mrs. Petty. He just hoped he wasn't going to be worse.

2

As soon as school was out, Walter tossed his notebook and speller over the fence and climbed into the Secret Passageway.

"Here we go again," he told Casey, who had gotten there ahead of him. "An autobiography. What a pain that's going to be."

"It could be a lot worse," Casey said. "Long division or something yucky like that." She picked up a stick and began to peel the bark.

Walter grunted and ripped a page out of his notebook. "I may as well get the autobiography out of the way first." He licked the point of his pencil, looked up in the air for a moment, then began to write.

Carrots, Walter's cat, leaped lightly to the top of

the fence. She stopped to wash one orange paw, then dropped from the fence into the Secret Passageway. Purring loudly, she rubbed herself against Walter's jeans.

"Hi, Carrots," Walter said. He leaned down to scratch the side of her neck and sighed. "Go away. Let me finish this."

Carrots seemed to know that Walter didn't have time for her, because she curled up near the other side of the fence, yawned once, and closed her eyes for a quick nap.

Walter wrote the last sentence. "Want to read this?" he asked Casey, handing her the paper.

Casey leaned back against the fence and read aloud:

THE LIFE OF WALTER MOLES (5)

I am ten and one-twelfth years old, not too short, not too tall. (19) I am mostly regular looking. I have brown hair and brown eyes. (31) I wear eyeglasses, that is, I wear them most of the time when they are not brocken or lost. My eyes are a little squinty looking when I take my glasses off. (63)

When I grow up I want to be a scientist. I have done a lot of experiments like inspecting dead fish and making doorbells and stuff like that. (91) The best experiment I ever worked on

THE END (100)

Casey handed back the paper. "You'll never get away with it."

"You'll never get away with it."

"Why not?" Walter asked.

"Stinks."

"He said a hundred words."

"You spelled *broken* wrong, and if you take my advice, you'll finish the last sentence and erase the numbers."

He grinned. "I didn't think there was a *c* in broken, but it looks funny without it." He slashed out the *c* with his pencil. Then he looked at the last sentence. "I ever worked on . . ." he muttered to himself. "Was . . . what?" He nodded to himself and wrote "is confidential." He crossed the *t* with a long line. "Just right," he said, pleased. "Now," he said, stretching, "spelling."

"How come you're doing your homework now?"

Walter opened his notebook to a new page. "My mother's on a school kick. Trying to make me into some kind of genius ever since she saw Mrs. Petty at the last P.T.A. meeting. I have to do all my homework before supper every night or I can't watch T.V."

"A genius? Mrs. Petty said you were that good?"

"Are you kidding? Of course not. She said I'd be a lot better off if I applied myself . . . handed in all my assignments."

Walter numbered from one to twenty-five on the page and began to write. "I like a . . . I hate a . . . I like a . . ." he mumbled as he wrote down the column.

Casey peered over his shoulder. "How do you get away with handwriting like that? So little and squiggly?" she asked. She put her face up to catch the sun. "Besides, you're supposed to use the spelling words in sentences."

"I am. I fill in the spelling words last. It makes it a little more interesting that way. Kind of a surprise in every sentence. Listen." He opened his spelling book. "The first word is *castle*. Okay. I like a *castle*. Two is *dress*. Okay. I hate a *dress*. Three is *throat*." He paused, pencil in the air. "Not too good. Can't like a throat," he muttered. "Unless maybe you're Dracula."

He slapped his pockets. "Lost my eraser again." He crossed out *I like* and stared into space. "Throat, throat," he whispered, looking through the fence into the schoolyard. "Look at that, will you?"

"Must be a zillion kids in there."

Walter nodded. "Whole world's gone baseball crazy. Half the kids in the fourth grade haven't even gone home yet. All they've thought about all day is that game with the fifth-grade team."

"That's good," Casey said. "The harder they work, the more chance we have of getting out of homework on Fridays." She stood up. "I'm a pretty good player myself." She bent over, picked up a small stone, wound up, and threw it through the Cyclone fence.

"Yes," she said, sinking down on the ground again, "I hit pretty well if I do say so myself. It's my catching that stinks."

"Well, that puts you ahead of me," Walter said, scratching a scab on his arm. "I stink at both."

He looked at the pail in back of him. "Talk about stink," he said. "Maybe we should give up on that water. Outside of those little string things floating around in there, nothing much seems to be happening. How about we start on something new?"

13

84-21

Casey got up and looked in the pail. "Maybe we should throw in some gunk. Help it along a little."

"Don't suppose we could use it for the science fair." He held up his hand. "Is that my grandmother calling?"

They both listened.

Mrs. Thorrien's voice floated toward them from Walter's back door. "Wal-tair. Wal-tair."

"Who else around here talks with a French accent like that?" Casey said. "I didn't know she was visiting you again."

Walter sighed. "I can't get one thing done around here without someone calling me. Yes, she's going to stay for a while. She has something wrong with her leg. Arthritis or something like that. Has to use a cane most of the time."

"Too bad," Casey said. "I hope she'll teach me some French words the way she did in the fall."

"I guess so," Walter began and broke off.

"Wal-tair. Wal-tair," Mrs. Thorrien called again.

Walter closed his speller. "Oh well," he said. "I didn't feel like doing that homework anyway." He stood up. "Yep. Gram is here all right. My mother moved me out of my bedroom and her right in." He grinned. "Good thing I'm easy to get along with. Besides, my father is going to give me a dollar for every week that I have to sleep in the laundry room."

He cupped his hands around his mouth. "Be right there," he shouted.

He put his foot through one of the holes in the fence and swung himself up. "See you tomorrow," he said. "I probably have to go to the store or something."

14

3

At dismissal the next day, the fourth-grade boys pounded down the gray metal stairs leading to the schoolyard. Walter trailed behind carrying two bats. Ahead of him, J.R. was bent nearly double under a blue canvas bag that held the balls and metal doughnuts for batting practice. J.R. was telling Charlie Eels about the Mets-Pirates game he had seen last summer.

Walter slung the bats off his shoulder and held them in his hands like canes so they'd thunk down the stairs. They made a terrific noise.

He raced back up the stairs to try it again.

J.R. yelled up at him. "Hey, Moles, what are you doing? By the time we get out to the field, we'll all have beards."

Walter peered through the railing. "I'm coming right now." He raced down the stairs, clunking the bats against each step.

Over his head on the second-floor landing, Mrs. Otto, the third-grade teacher, clapped her hands. "What's all this noise?" she asked.

Walter jumped. As he looked up, one of the bats slipped out of his hand and went between his legs. He tripped over it and slid down the last three steps, ramming into J.R. and Charlie.

They hopped around for a moment trying to keep their balance. Then they collapsed under the canvas bag.

"Hey, Charlie," Walter said as soon as they had untangled themselves. "I think you're bleeding."

Charlie heaved himself to his feet. "Split my lip a little," he said, feeling his mouth.

Above them Mrs. Otto's head appeared over the railing. "What's going on down there?" She stared at Charlie. "Get yourself home right now and put some ice on that lip," she said.

Charlie shook his head. "I've got to play ball." He wiped his chin, smearing the blood.

Mrs. Otto put her hands on her hips. "I want you to go home," she said. "Now."

Charlie opened his mouth. Then he looked at Walter.

"Listen, Mrs. Otto," Walter said, "it's my fault this happened. The kids are going to nail me to the wall if Charlie doesn't play. He's the best shortstop around. Without him . . ."

Mrs. Otto looked up at the ceiling. "It's just not possible," she said. "I'm worn out and these boys make

"Get home, young man," Mrs. Otto said. "Right now."

me repeat myself forty times before it finally sinks in."
She raised her voice. *"Get home, young man,"* she told
Charlie. *"Right now."*

The three of them stood there looking up as she
banged through the hall doors and disappeared.

"Maybe I could—" Charlie began.

"Don't be crazy," Walter said. "She'll probably
watch out the window. You'd better go home."

Charlie wiped his chin again. "Here, take my mitt,
Walt. Someone will need it." He crossed the schoolyard and headed for 199th Street.

"There goes the game," J.R. said.

Walter nodded slowly. He gathered up the bats,
walked out the door, and trotted over to the ball field
ahead of J.R.

There were about four little clumps of grass on the
whole field. The rest was all brown. On rainy days
most of the field turned into a mud puddle, but on days
like today it was as dry and hot as a mouthful of
pizza pepper.

Gunther Reed, the rest of the boys, and a few girls
were hunched on the ground leaning against the
schoolyard fence. They were watching the fifth graders
warm up.

"They're good, all right," Gunther told Walter. He
pointed toward the backstop. "Remember that guy
over there? His name is Samson. Everyone in his class
calls him Rat Teeth. He's some slugger, let me tell
you."

Walter glanced over toward Rat Teeth. He was
horrible. One of his yellow front teeth leaned over on

the other. And both teeth were so long that they didn't fit in his mouth.

Walter watched him for a minute. "You're right. He's good."

Clyde Warner, the fourth-grade catcher, looked up. "Maybe it's because they got here in time to get in some practice." He ran his hand across the top of his head and kicked one of Walter's bats. "That J.R. is a turtle. He told everyone he could carry most of the game stuff out by himself. Then it took the two of you forever to get outside. We've been sitting here for ten minutes counting airplanes."

Gunther Reed stood up. "No time to practice now." He looked around. "Hey, where's Charlie?"

Walter smoothed out a small mound of dirt with the toe of his sneaker. "Split lip," he said quietly. "I ran into him. Mrs. Otto sent him home."

"Home!" Gunther yelled. "Is she crazy? If Charlie's still breathing, he should be out here playing short-stop."

"Well, that's Mrs. Otto for you," Clyde said. "My dog is smarter than she is. And he isn't even house-broken. Goes to the bathroom all over the place."

Walter nodded. They were so worried about Charlie, they forgot to blame him.

"Will you stop talking garbage and let me figure out who's going to play shortstop?" Gunther screamed at Clyde. "Or do you feel like doing homework every Friday night for the rest of the year?"

"Take it easy," J.R. said. "Clyde has to catch. Put anyone else there and we'll spend the whole game waiting for the catcher to chase balls all over the field. I remember I saw an all-star game on T.V. once and—"

"Will you shut up," Gunther yelled. "Of course Clyde has to catch. Get out to left field while I figure the rest of this out. I'm sick of listening to you and your television and your movies—" He broke off. "Walter, you play shortstop."

"I was just going to watch," Walter said.

"I kind of thought I'd . . ." J.R. began.

"Good idea," Walter agreed.

"What about me?" Mitchell Marino yelled. "If it wasn't for my sister bringing in that note—"

"Shut up, Mitchell," Gunther said. "I'm sick of everybody trying to give orders around here. I'm the captain."

"Who said?" Mitchell screamed, throwing down his cap.

"I said." Gunther practically stuck his nose in Mitchell's face.

"I'll play shortstop," Albert Fein said.

Gunther threw up his hands. "Why doesn't someone run in and ask Mrs. Otto? Maybe she'd like to play shortstop."

Walter sat down on the ground. He was glad to be out of the whole thing. He just wished they'd make up their minds. By the time they started the game . . .

"I'm going home," Mitchell Marino said, "unless I play shortstop."

"Go ahead home," Albert said. "You stink anyway."

"How about I—" J.R. said.

"I said Walter is the shortstop," Gunther shouted. He turned to Walter. "I know you'd rather be fooling around with your experiments. But I remember you played once last year. You played first base or something . . ."

"Right field . . ." Walter began.

"You made a couple of catches. FAN-tastic."

"But Walter's left-handed—" J.R. began.

"What is this? Some kind of discrimination?" Gunther shouted. "I saw him make the best catches I ever saw. Right on this ball field."

J.R. shrugged. Gunther kept screaming.

Walter gulped. They were the only two catches he had ever made in his whole life. He had been thinking about something else and both times the ball had fallen right into his mitt. It could never happen again.

"Besides"—Gunther jabbed his finger toward 199th Street—"there goes Mitchell, the sore loser. And if you think I'm going to put J.R. at shortstop, you're crazy. If I have to listen to him gabbing all over the infield, I'm going to strangle him. He's told me about every television program that's been on since he was born. And the commercials too."

J.R. hitched up his pants. "I'm getting out to left field. Nobody ever listens to me. No sense hanging around all day. The other team is ready." He started across the field. "Everybody around here is in a lousy mood," he said over his shoulder.

"So how about it, Walt?" Gunther asked.

Walter hesitated. It was his fault that Charlie was home with an ice cube on his mouth. He guessed it was his fault too that the whole team was arguing.

"All right," he said finally. "I'll do it."

4

A hot wind blew across the infield, raising the dust and blowing some candy papers against Walter's feet.

Walter kicked them away and licked his lips. He was dying for a drink of water.

Out of the corner of his eye he could see Casey in the Secret Passageway. She was leaning against the fence, a can of soda in her hand, ready to watch the game.

He wished he was kneeling there too. He picked a couple of pebbles out of the dirt and threw them over his shoulder. That Gunther Reed was crazy, putting him at shortstop just because he had made those lucky catches last year. He shook his head. In about ten minutes Gunther would find out how bad he was.

He wiped his sweaty hands on his pants and looked at the batter's box.

Bobby Sanchez was up first for the fifth grade. He clunked the bat on the ground a couple of times, trying to look good. Gunther pitched a fast one and Sanchez popped out to Warner.

Donny Polik was up next. It seemed to take him forever to walk from the bleachers to the batter's box. And Gunther was in no hurry either. He kept straightening his cap and tossing the ball from one hand to the other.

Walter poked his glasses up on his nose and glanced over to the Secret Passageway again. Casey was bending over, looking into their experiment pail. He watched her stir up the muddy water. She bent over farther to get a closer look. He wondered if she had found . . .

Whish. Something flew by close enough for him to feel the breeze against his right ear.

It was the ball, heading for left field.

"Moles, you idiot!" Gunther screamed. "That ball was right in your pocket. How could you have missed it?"

Walter swiveled around. Gunther was jumping up and down on the pitcher's mound as the runner rounded first base.

In back of Walter, J.R. scrambled to pick up the ball. Too late. It bounced between his legs and rolled across the back of the field and under the schoolyard fence into the street.

"You jerk!" Gunther yelled at J.R. and threw his hat on the ground.

23

Rat Teeth was up, ready to swing.

By this time the runner was crossing home plate. J.R. tore out of the schoolyard to get the ball before some other kids out on the street grabbed it.

Rat Teeth hopped around, his stomach jiggling under his orange and white polo shirt. He was screaming about their home run.

Gunther was screaming too. Clyde took off the catcher's mask and walked toward the pitcher's mound. "Don't get so excited, Goony," Clyde called. "Game's just started."

"Sure, sure," Gunther yelled back. "Game's just started and they've got a home run. With goof-offs like we've got, the score'll be a hundred to nothing by the time we get out of here." He caught the ball that J.R., puffing back into the schoolyard, threw to him.

Walter stared at the ground. He picked up two pebbles and tossed them away from him.

"Psst. Moles. Walt," said a voice behind him. It was J.R., inching his way up from left field.

Walter moved back to see what he wanted. "I don't like to complain," J.R. half called, half whispered, "but you're making me look bad out here. I thought you had the ball for sure, so I didn't even bother to get ready for it. Next time look alive, will you, Moles?"

Walter wiped the sweat off the back of his neck and nodded. Then he looked over toward home plate. Rat Teeth was up, ready to swing.

Walter bent over, letting his arms hang loose. The batter popped a foul behind the catcher.

Clyde's little sister, Chrissy, was sitting in the dirt behind Clyde. She leaned over, caught the ball, and tossed it to him.

25

"Get out of there," Gunther yelled at her. "Want to get hit in the head?"

"Yeah," Clyde said as he threw the ball to Gunther. "Go on home, Chrissy."

She scrunched up her nose, stuck her thumb on the end of it, and waggled her fingers at them.

Walter grinned. Chrissy Warner was probably the toughest little kid in the neighborhood. She didn't worry about what anyone thought.

Gunther pitched again.

Crack. Rat Teeth connected with the ball. It sailed over Walter's head into left field.

J.R. waited for the ball to bounce toward him. He caught it, threw to second, but Rat Teeth got there first.

Now that Walter could see Rat Teeth up close, he looked even worse. Besides his awful teeth, his face was all sweaty and there was a jagged hole in his polo shirt. He looked like a mess. A tough mess.

Rat Teeth stared back at Walter. "You'd better shine up those glasses," he called. "You catch like a blind man."

Walter opened his mouth to answer, but he couldn't think of a thing to say. He turned back to the game and watched Gunther winding up on the pitcher's mound.

As the ball whizzed across the plate, Vinnie Patterson, the next hitter, socked the ball straight toward Walter.

Walter stepped forward, reached for it, and missed. The ball grazed his elbow. "Yeow," he yelled. He jumped up and down, waving his arm in the air.

Head down like a bull's, Rat Teeth rushed blindly for third base. Right into Walter's side.

"Oof." Walter felt the wind explode out of him. He fought to get his breath back.

By that time Rat Teeth was shouting, "Interference. You did that on purpose."

Walter opened his mouth. "I . . ."

"Did you see that?" Rat Teeth yelled. "The shortstop got in my way just so I couldn't get to third."

Gunther was jumping all over the place. "You're crazy," he screamed and barreled over to the two of them.

Rat Teeth balled up his fists and got ready to swing.

"Hey," J.R. yelled, "there's going to be a fight."

An upstairs window flew open and Mrs. Otto popped her head out. "Go home," she shouted. "You down there. Put those bats and things back into the gym and get off the field."

Everyone looked up at her.

"I mean it," she called. "If you can't play nicely, you can't play at all."

"Nicely!" Rat Teeth snorted.

Mrs. Otto leaned out a little farther. "What's your name, young man? You—in the orange shirt."

Rat Teeth ignored her. "Come on, gang. These kids can't play. The shortstop cheats. Let's get out of here."

"Wait a darn minute," Gunther yelled. "You can't get away with that. We can so play. And Walter doesn't cheat. He's the best shortstop around. He doesn't have to cheat."

Rat Teeth stuck his face an inch away from Gunther's. No one was paying any attention to Mrs. Otto, who was still hanging out the window.

"I'm coming right down there," she shouted. "If anyone is still on the field when I get there, he can just come back up to the classroom with me for an hour or two."

"We're going," Rat Teeth yelled to Mrs. Otto. "Right now." He turned to Gunther. "You really think that shortstop is so great?" He laughed. "Let's see. Tomorrow." He put his hands on his hips and stared at Walter.

Walter shuffled his feet around. "Gunther's right," he said. "I don't cheat." He hesitated, thinking fast. "But I can't play tomorrow. I have to go to uh . . ."

"I have guitar lessons tomorrow," Gunther broke in. "And the dentist the day after."

"Checkup on Friday," added Clyde.

"All right," Rat Teeth said. "How about next Monday?"

"Wait . . ." Walter began, but it was too late.

Gunther jammed his hat down on his head. "Monday," he said. "You'll see what a great shortstop Walter is. We'll be here. Waiting for you."

He turned to Walter. "It's up to you, Walt. The game and the homework. Don't let us down."

Walter opened his mouth. He stood there for a second, then closed it again with a little click.

28

5

Walter opened the back door and walked into the kitchen.

Mrs. Thorrien stood at the counter near the stove, dropping small pieces of dough onto a baking sheet. Her plump face was pinkish-red from the heat of the oven and her eyeglasses were steamy. She pushed back a piece of hair that dangled over her eyes. "You are late getting home from the school," she said.

"Baseball game," he answered. He wandered over to the table. He loved his grandmother's homemade bread. He picked up a knife and covered a thick slab of bread with butter.

"I am making cream poofs," his grandmother said. She reached for her cane, which was leaning against the counter, and hobbled over to the table. "I will tell you something, Waltair. It will be our secret. I am going to enter a cooking contest."

Walter stood up. "Good," he said, his mouth full of bread.

"*Oui.* And I am going to enter some poofs."

"Why don't you enter your bread?" Walter asked.

His grandmother made a face. "Bread is not special. Not fancy."

Walter shrugged and helped himself to another slice of bread and butter. Then he opened the door to the laundry room.

Inside, there was just enough room for the washing machine, the drier, and Walter's cot, which was wedged between the back wall and the table Mrs. Moles used to fold the clean clothes. A square of sunlight from the window over the cot shone on the pink tile floor.

Walter dropped his notebook and speller on top of the drier and threw himself down on the cot. He could hear the phone ringing in the front hall. He didn't move.

That Gunther Reed had gotten him into some mess. How could Goony say he was a great shortstop! How could he even think it?

Walter rolled over and stared at the ceiling. How could he get out of Monday's game? Maybe his father could help him practice, maybe he . . .

"Waltair," his grandmother called. She limped to the laundry room door and peered in. "Are you asleep?"

"Uh-uh," he answered.

"Ah, good." She wiped her hands on her apron. "Your mother has just called. Would you go to the hardware store? Bring your mother and father their supper? They are too busy to come home."

Walter nodded and swung his legs over the side of the cot. "I'll be ready in a second."

Five minutes later he was heading for Hollis Avenue carrying a bulging brown paper bag. It held thick ham sandwiches on his grandmother's bread, a couple of slabs of cheese, and three dill pickles that Walter could smell right through the bag.

He balanced the bag carefully with one hand as he opened the door to the hardware store with the other. It was dark and cool inside. He took a deep breath. He loved the rubbery smell he always noticed when he came into the store.

He passed counters of nails, and tools, and ropes of chain hanging from hooks, and nodded to some of the people waiting at the cash register to pay for their things.

Behind the counter his mother was packing cans of paint into a cardboard box. She had a ball-point pen stuck behind one ear and wore a big gray apron that said MOLES'S HARDWARE STORE. She waved to Walter. "Your father's in the back," she said.

Walter pushed aside the dark green curtain that led into the stock room. "Supper's here," he said to his father, who was up on a ladder reaching for a can on a shelf.

"Just spread it out, Walt," Mr. Moles said. "I'll be right down as soon as I get this can of solder for a customer."

Walter made a space on the table by pushing aside a bunch of papers with paint samples and some boxes of nails and bolts. Then he dumped everything out of the bag and unwrapped the dill pickles.

"Listen, Dad," he said. He took a bite out of one of the pickles and licked the juice that ran down his wrist. "I know you're busy, but I need some help."

Mr. Moles climbed down the ladder. "I'll be right back," he said, pushing the green curtain aside.

Walter went to the little refrigerator in the corner and took out a Coke.

A moment later his father was back. He sat on the edge of the table and picked up a sandwich. "What's doing?"

"How about we play a little baseball when you close up tonight?" Walter asked.

His father shook his head. "We're so busy tonight, we probably won't be finished before it's dark."

"How about the rest of the week?"

"Gee, Walter, I'd like to, but this is really a busy season for the store. Now that the good weather is really here, people are painting or fixing up their houses and they all need hardware supplies."

"How about Sunday?" Walter asked.

His father's face fell. "I promised Uncle Jack I'd help him paint the trim on his house. I'll be over there all day. I'm really sorry, Walt."

Walter looked down at the table and shrugged. "It's all right, Dad. Don't worry."

"What's the sudden rush to play ball, anyway?" his father asked.

"I have to learn how to be a great shortstop. Right away. Like before the weekend is up."

"You're right, Walt," Mr. Moles said. He took a bite of his sandwich. "You've got a problem."

"So maybe not a great shortstop. If I could just be a pretty good shortstop . . ."

His father waved his sandwich in the air and swallowed. "A pitcher, fine," he said. "A right fielder, all right. A first baseman, great. But not a shortstop."

Walter was puzzled. What was his father talking about?

"Didn't you know there's no such thing as a left-handed shortstop?"

"What difference does that make? Just because I'm left-handed . . ."

Mr. Moles reached for the brown paper bag and took a stubby yellow pencil out of his pocket. He drew a baseball diamond and jabbed at a spot between second and third base.

"Here's where a shortstop stands, Walt. Now watch." Mr. Moles jumped off the table and crouched down. "Suppose I want to put the runner out at first." He fielded an imaginary ball with his left hand, picked it out with his right, and threw it toward first. "Nothing to it. But that's because I played right-handed. My legs and arms were facing first base.

"Now watch me again. This time I'll try it left-handed." With his right hand, he reached across himself. "See how awkward it is to catch the ball in this position? And then when I finally get the ball into my left hand, I'm facing in the wrong direction. By the

33

"There's no such thing as a left-handed shortstop."

time I pivot around to throw to first, the runner's sitting on base laughing at me."

He threw his invisible cap into the air and sat down on the table again.

Walter looked at him incredulously. "You mean I can't be a shortstop?"

His father shook his head. "I think you'd better choose another position."

Walter gulped. "It's too late for that," he said slowly and picked up his sandwich.

6

"That Gunther Reed is crazy," Walter said to Casey as they crossed the schoolyard at dismissal time the next day.

"Goony's a lot of fun," Casey said, "but he certainly got you into some mess this time."

"My father says there aren't any left-handed short-stops. Too bad Goony didn't think about that before he began shouting all over the place how good I am."

"That's because Goony probably doesn't know any-thing about it," Casey said.

"Well, it's too late now," Walter said. "Let's go over to the park and hit some balls. I don't want the whole world to find out what a terrible player I am."

"I have to drop off my stuff first," Casey said, "and

let my mother know where I'm going." She tucked her history book under her arm and bent down to tie her sneaker. "I thought you were supposed to do your homework right after school."

"This is an emergency," Walter said. "I have to be a star shortstop practically overnight."

Casey looked up as they reached the schoolyard gates. "Hey," she said.

Walter stopped short. Coming slowly down the street, straight toward them, was his grandmother.

He grabbed Casey's arm and ducked back into the schoolyard. "She's supposed to have leg trouble," he said, "but she manages to get all over the place."

He shoved his glasses up on his nose. "I know just what she's going to say. 'Wal-tair. Be a good boy and get your homework done. I know you want to be a famous ecologist someday.'"

"You'd better stop talking," Casey said. "She'll be here any second."

"Tell her . . ." he began and stopped to think. "What?"

"Suppose I tell her you had to help the teacher after school? That you're going to be home a little late."

"Good. I'll go out the other gate and meet you in the park."

Casey nodded.

"While you're at it," Walter said, "tell her Mr. Dengle needs me to help him because I'm the smartest kid in the class. Or something like that. You know, to get her off my back about doing homework all the time."

Casey nodded again. "Got you."

"And don't forget to bring a—"

"I know," Casey broke in. "A bat and a ball."

"I'd better get going," Walter said. "Here she comes." He took off across the schoolyard, ran out the back gate, and raced down to the park on 196th Street.

A few little kids were running up and down the slides or sitting on the swings while their mothers sat on the benches watching them. One of the mothers looked up as Walter ran past her. She was knitting something that looked like a long pink and blue kite. "Hey," she called. "You. With the glasses."

Walter stopped running.

"Why are you racing around like that? Do you want to knock somebody over?"

Walter looked at the ground. Then the woman started to yell at a little girl who was bouncing up and down on the seesaw. Walter walked quickly toward the rear of the park.

He came to a grassy area near some tables where a bunch of old men played checkers every day. It was a great ball field, but most of the time the boys didn't play there. When they did, the men grumbled and carried on about the noise they were making. Once Goony had hit a ball that landed right in the middle of someone's checkers game, scattering the pieces all over the place. The men had complained to the guard and he had chased all the kids out of the field.

Walter looked around. There were only two or three men there. This was probably the best spot in the neighborhood for Casey and him to practice. Nobody would see him looking like a dummy. All the kids would be in the front of the park or back at the school-yard.

Walter walked on past the tables and sank down on the ground under a tree. He leaned back to look at the leaves and thought about telling Goony the truth. It would never work, he thought. Goony would have his hide for making him look like an idiot in front of the fifth graders.

Ten minutes later Walter saw Casey coming. She was dragging a bat along the cement walk. When she got near the tables, she lifted the bat so she wouldn't get the men mad about the noise.

"What did my grandmother say when she found out I wasn't coming home?" Walter asked as Casey squatted down next to him.

Casey shrugged. "She wasn't even looking for you. She said she was taking a walk. Exercising her leg. Taught me a French word too. *École*. Means school."

"Did you tell her I was helping Mr. Dengle?"

"Yes. She said, 'That Waltair is vary intelligent. I think he will be prasident someday.'"

Walter grinned.

"Come on, champ," Casey said. "Ready?"

Walter nodded. "Now look, Casey. Make believe you're at home plate. Hit some balls to me. See if I can catch them and slam them back to you."

"What good will that do?" Casey asked. "What you really have to practice is catching the ball, then turning toward first as fast as you can."

"I'm going to make believe you're at first base."

"That's no good," Casey said. "Not one bit authentic if I'm at home plate."

39

"Come on, champ," Casey said. "Ready?"

"Will you stop making such a thing about all this?" Walter said. "It's complicated enough as it is."

Casey shrugged and walked away from him. She tossed a ball into the air and batted it toward him.

Walter missed, and the ball flew toward the checkers table. "Don't worry," he told Casey. "Just need a little practice."

"Watch where you're throwing that ball," one of the men yelled as Walter ran past the checkers table to get the ball.

"We will," Walter promised. He threw it back to Casey.

She tossed the ball up in the air again and hit it toward him.

Walter reached for the ball, but it whizzed past him. A lot of practice, he thought.

"Terrific," Casey said as he watched the ball bounce between the trees. "A really fine catch by our star shortstop, Walter Moles."

Walter ignored her and ran for the ball.

This time when she hit it toward him, he caught it but fumbled and dropped it. He wiped his face with a corner of his shirt. "Let's rest awhile," he said. "This really isn't too easy."

"Rest?" she said. "You haven't been here for five minutes. How do you expect to be a great shortstop if you don't put some effort into it?"

"Yeah," he said. "Better hit one more." He stood there waiting for her to swing. A blue jay swooped down next to him and Walter watched it peck at something in the grass.

Casey walked over to him. "Listen, Walt, how do you expect to catch the ball if you're looking at a bird?"

Walter smiled sheepishly. "I was looking at that guy who just yelled at us. Did you notice he hasn't got one hair on his head?"

"What I notice," Casey said, "is that he's heading straight for us."

"Hey, kids," the bald man said. "What are you doing?"

Walter shrugged. "Just practicing a little."

The man had a toothpick stuck in the corner of his mouth. He wiggled it around a little. "Lousy catcher," he said. "Don't mean to hurt your feelings."

"That's okay. I know," Walter said. His feelings were a little hurt.

"He's practicing to be a shortstop," Casey said.

The man rolled the toothpick around in his mouth. "Left-handed, isn't he?"

Walter sighed. He knew what was coming.

"Never heard of a left-handed shortstop," the man said.

Walter looked at Casey. She shrugged.

"All right," said the man. "First time for everything. Name's Sonny. You get back at bat, young lady . . ."

Sonny! Walter tried not to laugh. The man looked about eighty years old.

"That's right. You get over there, young feller. That's first base. And I'll show you how to be a shortstop."

Walter trotted over to the edge of the field.

"Go ahead, young lady," Sonny yelled. "Sock it right out here. Watch me."

Casey threw the ball in the air and batted it.

42

"Little out of practice," Sonny said.

Sonny missed the ball. It soared over his head and bounced out of the field.

"Just run and get the ball, kid," Sonny called to Walter.

Walter raced back to the trees for the ball and tossed it to Casey.

This time she batted the ball as carefully as she could.

But Sonny missed again. "Little out of practice," he said.

The third time Sonny missed, Walter said, "I think I need a drink of water."

"Me too," Casey said.

"We have to get home now," Walter said. "My mother is probably looking for me."

"All right," Sonny said. "I'm a checkers player myself. That's my thing."

"Well, it was a good try," Walter said. "It really was a help."

"Maybe we can get together again," Sonny said. "I'll look for you."

Walter gulped and waved as Sonny went back to play checkers.

"That was some session," Walter said as they left the park.

"We'll have to find a new place to practice tomorrow," Casey said.

"At this rate," Walter said, "I won't get to be a decent ball player for ten years."

7

"I'll never be good enough to play shortstop by Monday," Walter said to Casey. They were sitting on his front steps after Mrs. Moles's usual Friday night supper.

Casey curled Carrots over her lap and scratched the cat's neck. "Maybe you could be sick."

"I wish I'd get hit by a car or something," Walter said, picking at the moss between the bricks. "Get some kind of strange disease that would keep me out of school for a year or two . . ."

"You'd miss the class trip to the art museum next week," Casey said.

Walter nodded. "And that trip's as good as a day off from school. Maybe I could break a leg."

"An arm would be easier."

"Very funny." He looked down at his arm. "Trouble is, I'm a coward when it comes to pain. Maybe I could make believe I have the flu for a couple of days."

Casey shrugged. "They'd just postpone the game." She lifted Carrots off her lap. "You're too hot," she said. "Sit next to me."

Walter closed his eyes. "I need more time. If I could practice every day, I'd be ready in a couple of weeks." He leaned over to pet Carrots. "Do you think they'd forget about the game after a while?"

Casey sat up straight. "What about the homework deal? I'm kind of counting on that."

Walter jumped off the steps and hobbled down the walk, clutching his arm to his chest. "I'd have to have a sling if I broke my arm," he muttered. "Keep it in my pocket. Whip it out after I left the house so my mother, the great detective, and her henchman, my grandmother, wouldn't know what's going on."

"We're not going to get out of homework anyway, if you're the shortstop." Casey stared at Walter's arm.

"Thanks."

"You need a cast," Casey said. "That's what I had when I broke my arm in kindergarten."

Walter hopped up on the step right on Carrots's tail. She yowled and jumped into the bushes next to the steps.

"Sorry," Walter said to the cat. "You've got it, Casey. A cast." He nodded. "Perfect." He sat down and thought for a moment. "Have to be the kind of cast I could take off," he mumbled. "Off and on. What to use? Cement? No."

46

"Plaster," Casey said.

"How could I get it off? Take too long to chip it away every day."

Casey got up from the steps. "Walt, I know just the thing." She jumped up and down on the pavement.

"Calm down, Casey. Holy moly, you'll have my grandmother out here trying to find out what's going on."

"Remember that papier-mâché stuff we made last year? Started with balloons and blew them up. I have the directions in my notebook."

"Let me think," he said. "Yeah. A long balloon. Arm-shaped. Wrap it with papier-mâché. Smack white paint over the darn thing. Pop the balloon and slide the old arm right in."

"No good. You can't just whip a cast out of your pocket."

Walter wrinkled his forehead. "I could keep it in the garage."

"You're going to need a good story to tell Mr. Dengle and the kids about how you broke your arm."

Walter clutched his arm again. " 'Oh, Walter,' " he said. " 'You poor thing. What? You say you saved that baby's life when you climbed up the tree after it? Held it and fell after you handed it into its mother's arms? You deserve a medal. Don't do any homework on Thursdays from now on.' "

"Yeah," Casey said. "Except how did the baby climb up a tree in the first place?"

Walter collected the pieces of moss he had dug out of the stoop and began to push them into a pile. "How about I jumped into the path of a speeding train to save an old man? Rolled out from under at the last minute?"

"Haven't you got any style at all, Walter?" She gazed off into space. "You were in your backyard. It was getting dark. You looked up into the sky and suddenly there were lights. Strange, glowing red and green lights. Flashing. 'Strange,' you said to yourself. 'It seems to be some sort of flying thing.' Then suddenly . . ."

"Casey, nobody will ever believe I was attacked by a UFO."

"How about a noise? Yes, a crashing noise. In the inky blackness of your basement. 'A good thing,' you said to yourself, 'that I don't mind being completely alone in the house.' Bravely you inched your way down the stairs. Suddenly you saw something, a shape strangely like an alligator's tail . . ."

"Why don't we figure that part out after we make the cast? It'll probably take us the whole weekend." He slapped his pockets. "Good thing the school lunch was some kind of dog-food junk today. I didn't buy any, so I can use my lunch money."

"For what?"

"I'm going to the ten-cent store. To buy some balloons. The long kind." He stopped. "Don't bother to come with me. We've got a lot to do. Get your notebook from last year and round up all the newspapers you can find. I'll meet you in my garage."

Casey waved and dashed across the lawn to her house.

"And Casey?" Walter called over his shoulder.

She paused on the steps.

"Close the garage door after you're in. If my grand-mother sees you, she'll be dying to know what you're doing. That's one woman who isn't happy unless she knows every single thing that's going on in the whole city."

Walter raced down to the corner, crossed the street diagonally, and turned up 201st Street. Halfway up the block, in front of J.R.'s house, he stopped to catch his breath.

J.R. came around the front of his house. He had a book in his hand. He waved it at Walter. "Hi, Moles," he said. "I'm studying up on baseball. Trying to mem-orize the names of all the men who made the Hall of Fame."

Walter grunted.

"Do you want to catch a few?" J.R. said. "Get the old wing in shape for Monday's game?"

"Not now, J.R., I've got some other things I have to do. Some other time." He started to run again.

"I hate to tell you, Moles, but that's your whole trouble. How are you ever going to be a great baseball player . . ."

Walter didn't hear the rest as he raced down the block and crossed the street.

8

Ten minutes later Walter slid up his garage doors, ducked under, and pulled them down behind him.

Casey was crouched on the cement floor, surrounded by papers, looking through her old notebook. She pushed her bangs out of her eyes. "This certainly is the cleanest garage in the world," she said.

Walter looked around. "That's because my father never bothers to put the car in here. We'll have all weekend to get the cast ready."

"I haven't found the directions yet. I'm sure it's in this book though. Somewhere."

Walter looked over her shoulder and read out loud as she paged through. "HOW TO MAKE A VOL-CANO. Might be good for a science project."

"Nah," Casey said. "Everybody's done one of those. You can get it out of any old science book in the library."

"HOW TO DISSECT A WORM. Remember when we did that last year?"

"I remember how it didn't work. Just looked like a couple of smaller worms when we got through."

Walter pushed his glasses up higher on his nose. "Here it is," he said. "Still has glue all over the page. He picked it up and read aloud:

DIRECTIONS FOR PAPER-MACHE

by

MOLES AND VALENTINE

Take some flour. Mix with water. Not too much. Not too little. (Otherwise turns into a glob or too runny.) Take something for underneath like a balloon. Blow up until big enough for what you want. Cut strips of newspapers into small pieces. Like about as big as a candy bar. Soak in flour glue. Start to paste on balloon. Keep pasting till the whole balloon is covered. It will be messy looking and very wet. As soon as you're finished with the first layer you can start with the second layer. So use comic strips for the second layer. (Otherwise you can't tell which layer is which.) Wait till this dries. Then put on two more layers. Wait again till it dries. Then the last two layers.

P.S. Do not leave in a damp place like cellar or Secret Passageway because it doesn't dry and just gets smelly and mothers make you throw it out.

"Okay," Walter said. He opened the brown paper bag from Bongo's Ten-Cent Store and pulled out a package of balloons and a small jar of white paint. "Everything we need," he said, "except for the flour. And that may be a little bit of a problem."

"I know what you mean. We're going to have to get some right out from under your mother's nose."

"Nah, she's working at the store tonight. It's my grandmother. She spends her whole life sitting in the kitchen. She's so close to the flour, she could practically hatch it."

Casey giggled. "So what are we going to do? Can't get it out of my house. My sister Van's in the kitchen with Sue Verona. They're making pineapple surprise cookies." She made a face. "I don't know why they bother. They taste like yuck."

"I guess we'll have to try my grandmother," Walter said. "Come on." He pushed up the garage doors and crossed the backyard in front of Casey.

"Keep your fingers crossed," he said. They stamped up the three steps to the kitchen door.

Walter's grandmother was sitting at the table chopping onions with a long, sharp knife. She put the knife down when she saw them, tucked a wisp of brownish-gray hair behind her ear, and smiled at them.

"Waltair and Casee," she said. "Have you hungair?"

Walter sidled over to the flour canister on the counter. "No," he said, "not really. Though actually we could take a piece of cake, or some bread. I just have to get a little flour for something."

Mrs. Thorrien nodded. "For what?"

"For what?" Walter repeated.

"For what?"

"Because I have just a little hunger," Walter said, looking at Casey, who was trying hard not to laugh.

"How are you?" Casey said. "I mean, *Comment allez-vous, Madame Thorrien?*"

"*Très bien,*" Mrs. Thorrien said, "except for the hip, which is not *très bien* at all."

As casually as he could, Walter lifted the cover off the flour canister and reached for a large bowl with his free hand.

"Waltair. What are you doing?"

Walter jumped. "Oh. I'm taking a little flour. For a project." He tilted the edge of the canister and started to guide the flour into the bowl with his fingers.

"*Sacre bleu,*" said his grandmother. "Is that the way you handle food? With the filthy fingers? I wanted to use that flour to make the cream poofs."

"I'll get a spoon right away."

Mrs. Thorrien stood up. "What kind of a project?"

"It's for school," Walter said, crossing his fingers and trying to pick up a spoon. "You know these teachers. Always homework projects."

"There is the phone now," Mrs. Thorrien said. "It is for me, I think. The doctor about my leg medicine." She hobbled across the kitchen floor toward the hall. "*C'est fou,*" she said over her shoulder. "You poor children. When I went to school, we did sensible things like reading and arithmetic. Now is the space age. Flour projects." She disappeared into the hall.

Walter dropped the spoon and scooped a heap of flour out of the canister with the side of his hand, then patted it down even with the top of the bowl. "Come on," he told Casey. He licked his fingers and wiped them over the floury counter top.

"There's more on the floor," Casey said.

"This stuff really gets all over the place, doesn't it?" He shuffled his feet to spread the flour around a little. "Can't see it now," he said. "Hold the door open. Let's get out of here before my grandmother gets back and sees how much we took."

He slipped out the door ahead of Casey, holding the bowl in front of him, then hurried across the yard and waited for her to open the garage doors.

Once inside, they looked at each other. "Ready?" Casey asked. She knelt down and began to tear the newspaper into strips.

Walter stood there considering. "Right. Just let me get the hose to wet the flour down and a branch from one of the bushes to stir it with. I'll be right back."

A minute later he ducked into the garage again, dragging a dripping hose behind him. He dangled it across the bowl, watching as the water made a lake in the mound of white flour.

"Enough water," he said, stirring the paste gently with the branch. He ran back to the garage door and threw the hose onto the driveway.

"You're getting paste all over the place," Casey said.

Walter zigzagged the branch through a dollop of thick flour water and wiped it off on the edge of the

"Here we go," Walter said.

bowl. Then he knelt over the bowl and stuck his fingers in it. "Just right." He held his fingers up in the air, curved and coated with paste. "Is that you, Count Dracula?" he asked in a deep voice. "Something terrible has happened to your hands."

Casey laughed, and he wiped his hands on the newspaper. "Now just make a balloon arm and we'll be able to paste."

Walter picked up the package of balloons. "Let's try a red one," he said and tore the cellophane bag open with his teeth. He fished out a balloon and began to blow it up, stopping occasionally to measure it against his forearm.

"What do you think?" he asked finally.

Casey looked at it carefully. "I think it looks better than your own arm."

"I guess you think today's your funny day," he said. He picked up a piece of newspaper and dipped it into the flour paste. "Here we go," he said and stuck the first piece on the balloon.

9

At lunchtime the next day Walter had his cream cheese and jelly sandwich at the kitchen table, then wandered outside to sit on the front steps. He had nothing to do. Casey had gone shopping with her mother, and he had to hang around for the next ten minutes until the cast had dried enough for the third layer.

He nodded to Mr. Valentine, who was trimming the bushes in front of his house. Mr. Valentine had a transistor radio on his lawn blaring out a baseball game.

He just couldn't get away from baseball, Walter thought. Every time he turned around, there it was, hanging over his head. On the radio someone must have hit a home run. Walter could hear the crowd screaming. Mr. Valentine stopped clipping and tilted his head over to one side so he wouldn't miss anything.

Walter reached up and broke a branch off the bush next to him. He swished it around to ward off a fly that was determined to get into his ear. Then he stood up. He might as well do some of his homework. It was an ecology experiment. He thought about it for a minute, then he went into the house and brought out a jar with a cork stopper, a couple of plastic tubes, and a piece of netting.

He had just started to set everything up on the stoop when J.R. came up the front path. "Hey, Walter," he shouted, "get out the old mitt. Let's get a couple of swings in."

"In a little while," Walter said. He held up the cork and peered at the two holes he had bored in it the other day.

"What are you doing?" J.R. asked.

"Making a pooter," Walter answered. "Hand me a piece of that tube, will you, J.R.?"

J.R. reached for a piece of plastic tubing, gave it to Walter, and leaned over his shoulder. "What's a pooter?"

Walter pushed the tube through one of the holes in the cork. "Insect collector. Very important for ecologists." He grabbed another piece of tube and put it in the other hole in the cork. "Now look. All you have to do is stick the cork in the bottle. Then you put one tube over a bug and suck on the other tube. Whoosh. The bug is pulled up into the bottle."

J.R. laughed. "Suck too hard and you'll have the bug right in your mouth."

Walter sighed. "That's what the net is for, J.R. You stick that over the tube first."

J.R. shook his head. "Seems like an awful lot of trouble when you can just pick up the bug with your two fingers."

"Not if it's a black widow spider, or something really dangerous, J.R." Walter held up the bottle. "That's what ecologists have to face."

"Neat," J.R. said. He looked bored. "How about some baseball? I've been practicing all morning. Took a bunch of balls and batted them down my driveway, one at a time. Trouble was, I had to keep running after them."

"I'll play later," Walter said, thinking about the cast in the garage.

"If we're going to beat those guys on Monday, we'd better get practicing. I called for Gunther and Clyde before I came over here, but Gunther had to go to his aunt's wedding and Clyde is stuck in front of the T.V. watching some quiz game. So it's us, Walt. The honor of the fourth grade depends on us."

Walter snorted. "I can see the two of us, running around after the ball, pretending we're a whole team."

J.R. jumped off the step and began to do push-ups on the walk. "Well, what are we waiting for? Are we going to sit here all day like a bunch of celery? Doing nothing?"

"In a while." Walt adjusted one of the tubes. "I think I'll put some rubber over this. Make it tighter."

"The fifth graders are practicing in the schoolyard," J.R. said. "I guess they'll end up winning."

Walter sighed. "Maybe we should take a look at them. Check out their weak points."

"Yeah," J.R. agreed. "Maybe you should get your mitt and we can—"

"Nah. Let's go around the block. Sneak into Mrs. Tutty's backyard and watch from behind her bushes."

"You mean spy on them?"

"You got it, J.R. That's just what we'll do. But first I have to take care of something." He stood up. "I'll be right back."

Halfway around the house, he hesitated. J.R. was right behind him. "How about waiting on the steps?" Walter asked. "My father isn't too crazy about having everybody in the garage."

"What's in there?"

"Some of my father's stuff," Walter said vaguely.

J.R. nodded wisely. "Stuff for the hardware store, I bet."

Walter didn't say anything. He waited until J.R. went back toward the steps.

Cautiously Walter pushed the garage doors up about a foot and slid under. He glanced back to make sure J.R. couldn't see the cast laid out in the middle of the garage floor.

It was beginning to look like something, he thought, running his fingers over the top of the damp cast. It needed a few more layers to make it solid.

He bent over and tore a piece of the comics into strips. He stopped to read *Peanuts* but the last two pictures were missing. He sorted through the strips trying to match them. None of them seemed to fit.

Finally he gave up and looked at the flour paste in

60

"Why are you lying on the floor?" J.R. asked.

the bowl. It wasn't as runny today as it had been yesterday. Now it looked like a big grayish blob. He picked up the tree branch. As he started to stir, he looked at the garage floor. It was a good thing his mother didn't go there very often. Soggy pieces of newspaper were all over the place and a lot of the paste had dripped over the side of the bowl. It was stuck to the floor like cement.

Behind him something rustled. Walter jumped and swiveled around. Carrots, tail high, slipped into the garage. Behind her Walter spotted a pair of feet. He dove flat on the floor to cover the cast as J.R. bent down to see under the garage door. As he did, the bowl tipped. Walter could feel the sticky paste spreading across his shirt. He gritted his teeth.

"Why are you lying on the floor in there?" J.R. asked.

Walter eased himself off the top of the cast a little. "I had a little fall," he said. "Why don't you go out in front?" He crossed his fingers. "I think I heard someone calling. Maybe it was Clyde."

"Hurry up," J.R. said. His head disappeared and Walter watched his legs move out of sight down the driveway.

Carefully he stood up. The cast seemed to be all right. He scooped as much of the paste as he could off his shirt, then he mopped up the rest on the floor with strips of newspaper and stuck them to the cast.

"A little more as soon as I have time," he told Carrots, "and it will really be in good shape." He rubbed his wet hands on the back of his jeans and raced out of the garage.

10

"I'm ready now," Walter said as he turned the corner of the house.

J.R. looked up. He was doing push-ups on the front walk again. "About time," he grumbled. "What's that white stuff all over you?"

Walter dabbed at his shirt. "Knocked something over. It's nothing."

"What do you say we run?"

"To Mrs. Tutty's? A half block? Why?"

"Get the legs in shape for running bases. Strengthen them." J.R. ran around Walter in circles, lifting his legs as high as he could.

"Not a thing wrong with my legs," Walter said. He shook his head as J.R. ran up the block toward Mrs.

Tutty's ahead of him. It was the catching and the batting and that whole left-handed business that he had to worry about.

He caught up with J.R. and straddled the fire hydrant at the corner. Two doors down was Mrs. Tutty's house. It was bigger than most of the other houses on the block and behind the bushes in her yard was a terrific view of the playing field, even better than the view from the Secret Passageway.

Walter looked at the front of Mrs. Tutty's house carefully.

"What do you think?" J.R. asked.

"It's pretty dangerous," Walter said. "If we get caught, she'll carry on."

Walter looked at the windows along the side of the house. Even though the shades were down, Mrs. Tutty was probably waiting somewhere, ready to pounce on anyone who sneaked up her driveway. Ever since last year, when someone threw a wad of chewing gum over the schoolyard fence and hit her on the neck by mistake, she was very cranky.

Walter took off his glasses and wiped them on his shirt. "I hope she isn't in her yard fooling with her flowers," he said. "If she is, we're dead."

J.R. shrugged. "We have to take that chance."

With his fingernail Walter scratched at a bit of flour that was stuck to his glasses. "I tell you what," he said, holding the glasses up to the light and squinting at them. "We'll go up the driveway as quietly as we can and peek around the corner before we go through to the back. Follow me."

Walter took a deep breath and shot up the driveway

on tiptoes. He ducked his head between his shoulders as he skirted around the cement steps at the kitchen door, then stopped short at the corner of the house to listen. He thought he heard Mrs. Tutty rattling some dishes inside. J.R. was right in back of him, breathing down his neck. "Get off," Walter whispered. "I'm dying of the heat." He peered around the side of the house to make sure it was safe.

"It's all right," he whispered. "She's in the kitchen, I think." He tore across the yard, stepped through Mrs. Tutty's roses, and crawled under her sticker bushes.

He lay down flat next to the Cyclone fence. It was almost on top of the third-base line. He wiggled around to get comfortable. There was a scratchy line of blood on his hand from one of the stickers. He sucked at it as J.R. crawled in behind him.

"What did I tell you?" J.R. said. "Practically the whole fifth grade is here. And we've got a great spot. We're so close to home plate, we could spit on the catcher."

"Shut up, will you, J.R.," Walter whispered. "You want them to hear you?"

For a moment J.R. was quiet. Then he leaned closer to Walter. "Reminds me of a movie I saw. About these two F.B.I. agents . . ."

"Holy moly, J.R. Do you have to be such a pest? Keep quiet and let me see what's going on." Walter rested his chin in his hand. The fifth grade was divided into two teams. Rat Teeth, the catcher, danced back and forth on first base as Bobby Sanchez stepped up to bat.

Walter watched as Rat Teeth bent down to rub

65

"We're so close, we could spit on the catcher."

his hand in the dirt, then wipe it off on the back of his pants. He was filthy.

He was loud too. He yelled directions to the batter and told the pitcher how rotten he was. In between he cackled at the other players and whistled.

Walter put his head down and listened.

"Oh yeah, oh yeah," Rat Teeth yelled. "You gotta connect, Bobby baby. Pitcher's no good. You can do it, baby. You're going to connect."

Suddenly Rat Teeth was quiet. Walter raised his head in time to see him stare intently at the pitcher. Then he danced right off first base and tore for second. The catcher reached for the ball as it whizzed past Bobby and threw it toward second with all his might. He missed the second baseman by a mile. Rat Teeth crossed second and raced for third as the pitcher jumped up and down screaming, "Get the ball! Somebody get the ball!"

J.R. began to laugh but stopped. Rat Teeth, safe on third, was facing Mrs. Tutty's yard. "Who's there?" Rat Teeth yelled. "Time," he screamed to the umpire. "Somebody's spying on us."

"So what," the pitcher called back. "Let's play."

Rat Teeth turned back to yell at the pitcher, and Walter and J.R. raced out of the bushes and across the yard. Mrs. Tutty was coming out of the kitchen door with a bag of garbage in her hands.

Walter called hello as he sped past her but they didn't slow down until they reached Walter's front steps.

"Well," said Walter, "that was a big waste of time. We didn't find out a thing, and Mrs. Tutty is probably on the phone right now waiting to tell my grandmother I was in her yard." He lay back against the step. "It's a good thing Gram is a little hard of hearing or I'd probably get killed."

He reached down and picked Carrots up off the walk. "The fifth graders didn't look so hot, did they?"

J.R. sat down on the step next to him. "Don't kid yourself, Walt. Rat Teeth is about the best player in the neighborhood. And we've got to beat him." He picked up Walter's pooter. "Can I try it?"

Walter shrugged. "Go ahead."

J.R. put one piece of the tube over an ant that was scurrying around on the step, and put the other piece in his mouth. He took a deep breath, sucking in his cheeks. Then he took the tube out of his mouth and held up the bottle.

The ant was trapped inside. "It works, Walt," he said. "It really works."

"I thought it would," Walter said.

"I wish I had something that good to write up."

Walter thought for a moment. "Take it. It's yours."

J.R. hopped off the steps. "You're really a friend. I won't forget about this."

Walter grinned as he watched J.R. running down the street. It was worth the experiment to have a few minutes by himself to finish up the cast. Besides, there were a million more ecology experiments he wanted to try.

11

A strange whirring noise seemed to come from right under Walter's ear. "Don't shoot," he mumbled and sat up in bed. Carrots opened one eye and glared at him. Then she jumped off the bed and, holding her tail high in the air, disappeared down the stairs.

Outside it was just about light. Walter shook his head a couple of times to clear it, but the noise continued.

Finally he remembered. He had buried the alarm clock under his pillow to muffle the sound. He and Casey had a lot to do before school this morning, and the last thing they needed was his mother panting over their shoulders.

He fished around under his pillow for the clock, pulled it out, and turned off the alarm. Six o'clock. He yanked on his jeans and a shirt and tiptoed down the stairs after Carrots.

In the kitchen he stuck his head in the refrigerator. Nothing there worth eating except a bunch of flat cream puffs left over from last night's supper. He grabbed two of them on his way out.

He pushed up the garage doors. Casey had beaten him there. She was kneeling on a piece of dirty newspaper in front of the cast.

He looked around. The garage was even messier than he remembered. Torn newspapers littered the floor. Globs of floury water and drops of white paint were everywhere.

Walter held out a cream puff. "Strawberry whipped cream filling." He stuffed the other one in his mouth. "Taste terrible, don't they? Soggy. My grandmother's just learning how to make them."

Casey took a bite and shrugged. "Bad news, Walt," she said and pointed to the cast. "It's sopping wet." She ate the rest of her cream puff. "Pretty good. The cream puff, I mean."

Walter poked at the cast gently. He took his glasses out of his pocket, pushed them up on his nose, and studied the white paint smeared on his hand. Then he dabbed at a smudge of paint on his glasses.

"It's as wet as it was last night when we painted it." He shook his head in disgust.

"I told you we shouldn't paint it while the papier-mâché was still damp," Casey said.

"You were right," he said. He leaned over and sniffed at the cast. "Smells a little moldy or something."

"Maybe you could wear a white shirt today. Then nobody would notice if it smudged." She sniffed at the cast. "And you could use a dab of your father's aftershave lotion to get rid of the smell."

"Listen, Casey. Do you want to know what will happen if I wear this thing into school today? I'll tell you what'll happen," he said, not waiting for an answer. "Some idiot will want to autograph it. It'll be like signing wet toilet paper."

"I guess we'll have to skip the whole thing," Casey said, disappointed. "It would have been such fun too."

Walter broke in. "Have you gone soft in the head? That baseball game is scheduled for three o'clock this afternoon." He poked at the cast again. "Do you want me to look like an idiot on that field? Nobody in the fourth grade will be talking to me for the rest of the year." He closed his eyes. "Let me think."

"There's nothing to think about," Casey said. "The only way you can wear this cast to school is to get it dry somehow."

Walter opened his eyes. "I know that. I'm trying to think of how." He snapped his fingers. "Hair drier. You know, the kind that looks like a gun. We can blow it dry."

"My sister Van had one. I dropped it last week. Sparks all over the place." She swished air through her braces. "Doesn't work anymore. Van's mad as the devil."

"We don't need yours. My mother has one. She

keeps it in the bathroom, in the cabinet under the sink."

"Run and get it," Casey said. "It's still early. I'll clean the garage while you dry the cast."

"And what will we use to plug the drier in? Your ear?"

"Don't waste time being a smart aleck," Casey said. "You'll just have to do it in the house. Hurry up and get going."

Gingerly Walter picked up the cast. "Open the door, will you, Casey? I need both hands for this."

Casey pushed the garage door up high enough for Walter to duck under.

"Be right back," he said over his shoulder and scurried for the back door. Two minutes later he was back. "Hey," he whispered as loud as he could. "Let me in."

Casey opened the door again. "What's the matter?"

"Locked myself out." He put the cast on the garage floor. "It would be easier to break into Fort Knox than get into my own house. Good thing my father doesn't worry about the second floor. Bathroom window's probably open. I'll get a ladder and—"

"Are you crazy?" Casey exploded. "Do you know how high up that is? You'll probably end up with a real cast."

"I have to, Casey," Walter said. "I told you I can't go to school today without a broken arm. Now stop talking about it. Hold the cast, will you?"

He dragged the ladder out of the garage, across the yard, and leaned it against the side of the house. "Listen, Casey," he whispered, "don't make any noise." He put his foot on the bottom rung. "Hand me the cast and hold on to the bottom of the ladder to steady it. I'll kind of hold the cast with one hand and balance it against the ladder with my chest."

"How will you manage when you reach the top?" she whispered back.

Walter shrugged. "Who knows. I'll think of something by that time. Hold my glasses. If I break them again, my mother will kill me."

He inched his way up the ladder. It seemed to take forever. Even though he knew Casey was holding the bottom as tightly as she could, the whole ladder wobbled every time he took a step.

Finally he was almost to the top. He could see the rising sun glistening on the windowpane above him. He reached up and rested the cast on the sill.

He tried not to look down. Instead, he stuck his head up over the edge of the sill.

He looked straight into his grandmother's face.

"*Sacre bleu*," she screeched and hobbled out of the bathroom, slamming the door behind her. "James," she yelled to Walter's father. "Come quickly. There's some kind of animal trying to get into the bathroom window."

Walter slid open the screen, pushed the cast in ahead of him, and climbed in through the window. Dropping the cast into the tub, he opened the bathroom door. His father was pounding down the hall. "Out of my way, Walter," he roared. "Something's trying to get in the window."

Walter blocked the way. "Nothing out there, Dad. I think Gram was dreaming." He looked down the hall

"There's an animal trying to get into the bathroom."

to his grandmother, who was smoothing down her hair with trembling fingers. "You were probably half-asleep. Right, Gram?"

Mrs. Thorrien shook her head, confused. "You may be right, Waltair. I thought I saw a long, white leg in the window and two eyes . . . squinty, horrible little eyes." She shuddered. "Yes. Dreaming. I think I will go back to bed for a while."

"Good," said Walter's father. "We'll all go back to bed." He looked at Walter. "Why are you dressed at this hour of the morning? It's not even seven o'clock yet."

"Trying to get to school early," Walter answered.

His father nodded. "Good to see you thinking about school for a change." He turned and walked back to his bedroom.

Walter went into the bathroom and locked the door behind him. Poking his head out the window, he whispered down to Casey, "All right up here. Go clean the garage."

Humming, he turned the cold water faucet on full blast in the sink. Noisy as anything, he thought. He reached for the drier, plugged it in, and began to shoot the hot air over the cast to dry it.

12

After breakfast Walter said good-bye to his father and mother as they left for work. Then he raced back upstairs to his bedroom, closed the door behind him, and dragged the cast out from under his bed.

"Dry as an old bone," he told himself with satisfaction. He turned the cast so he could see the red balloon sticking out of the end. "I'll just pop this and try the whole thing on for size."

He poked at the balloon experimentally with his finger, first gently, then a little harder. Glancing at his desk, he saw a black ball-point pen. He reached for it and held it in the air for a second, aiming it. Then he shouted, "Bombs away," and jabbed it into the balloon as hard as he could. It exploded with a bang.

Downstairs his grandmother screamed.

He picked the pieces of red rubber out of the cast and dropped them into his pocket. By this time his grandmother was at the bottom of the stairs.

"Waltair," she shouted. "What is going on up there?"

Walter opened the door and looked down at her. "Nothing."

"What is the bang?"

"The bang," Walter repeated. "Oh, you mean that noise."

"*Oui.*"

"I just stepped on a little balloon. By mistake."

His grandmother wrinkled her forehead.

"Nothing to worry about," he said. "It happens all the time."

"Are you ready for the school?" his grandmother asked.

"Just getting ready now," he answered and closed his door again.

He picked up the cast. "Which arm?" he muttered. "Right or left?" It probably didn't make one bit of difference. A broken arm was a broken arm. He couldn't play baseball either way. He stood there considering. If he covered his left arm, he probably wouldn't have to do written homework. He nodded to himself and pulled the cast over his left arm.

It was a perfect fit. He checked it out in the mirror. He'd have to stick a little gauze in the end near his wrist, he thought critically. It was just a speck loose.

He cradled his left arm with his right and smiled bravely at the mirror.

"General," he said, "the enemy couldn't get the in-

77

formation from me. Oh, this? Nothing serious. They tore the arm out of the socket. Good thing I had medical training. I was able to push it back in and—"

The clock in the hall chimed once. Eight thirty.

Walter grabbed his books and left the bedroom. He checked the bottom of the stairs. His grandmother had gone. He raced down the hall and took a roll of gauze out of the medicine cabinet. Quickly he wound it around his wrist, stuffing the ends into the cast.

He tiptoed down the stairs. "See you later, Gram," he yelled and ducked out the front door.

Outside Casey was waiting for him.

"What do you think?" he asked, holding out his arm.

"Absolutely professional," she said, poking some loose gauze up inside the cast.

"It does look pretty good," Walter said as they started up the street for school. "It's a little soft on the top, but that's all right. The only thing wrong is the smell."

Casey breathed in as hard as she could. "It doesn't smell the way it did this morning," she said thoughtfully. "It smells more like . . ." She hesitated. "More like . . ."

"Sweet Violet Air Freshener," he said.

They turned in at the schoolyard gate. "I sprayed the whole thing with it after I dried the cast this morning."

"I was going to say," Casey said, "it smells like a bunch of dead flowers."

"My grandmother sprays it all over the place. In her dresser, the bathroom, her pocketbook . . ."

At the other end of the schoolyard, the fourth-grade boys were playing keep-away. J.R. Fiddle pointed at Walter.

"Hey, look at Moles!" J.R. shouted. "He's injured."

A minute later Walter was surrounded. As everyone jostled each other to get a look at his cast, Walter tried to cover it with his right arm.

"What happened?" Gunther Reed asked.

Walter looked at Casey. "Uh," he said. "I was uh . . ."

Casey giggled.

"You shouldn't laugh," J.R. told Casey. "It's not funny. A thing like this could probably kill a person. Blood poison and all . . ."

"Smells like the doctor put some strange medicine on it." Gunther broke in. "How did you do it anyway, Moles?"

"I . . ." Walter started again.

"Fell out of a tree?" Casey suggested.

"Yes," Walter repeated. "I fell out of a tree last night."

"Rescuing . . ." Casey prompted.

Walter frowned. "Rescuing er . . . rescuing . . ."

"Well, go ahead, Moles," Gunther said. "Don't be modest. If you're some kind of a hero, let us know about it."

Walter hesitated. "I really don't want to talk about it," he said finally and glared at Casey.

"How come you don't have a sling?" Gunther asked.

Walter looked at Casey. Her eyes widened.

"A sling," he said. "Yes. The doctor said . . ." he began. "The latest treatment . . . uh . . ."

"The doctor said," Casey cut in, "that for injuries

79

like that a sling is no good." She turned to Walter. "Isn't that what he said?"

Walter nodded.

For a minute everyone was quiet. Then Gunther put his arm around Walter. "I don't want to make you feel worse," he said, "but did you remember that this afternoon is the big game with the fifth-grade team?"

Walter looked at the ground. "Yes. I really feel . . ."

"I don't suppose the cast will be off by three o'clock," Gunther said.

Walter shook his head. "I guess you'll have to play without me."

"Not a chance," Gunther said. "How long before the cast comes off? A couple of days?"

Walter looked up. "No. Maybe three weeks. Two, if I can get in shape by that time."

"Get in shape?" Gunther asked.

"He means," Casey broke in quickly, "if he can get the doctor to take the cast off by then."

Gunther still looked puzzled.

Walter glanced at his fingers sticking out of the end of the cast. "Look," he said. "I can't move my fingers. As soon as I can wiggle them again, the doctor says the cast can come off."

Gunther stared at Walter's hand, fascinated. "Give it a little try, Moles."

Walter held out his arm. Pretending to concentrate very hard, he looked at his fingers. Finally he sighed. "Nothing."

Gunther look disappointed. "J.R. is right, Walt. Keep trying. Maybe there'll be a miracle and you can play today."

"I doubt it," Walter said, trying to sound disappointed. "What about Charlie Eels? He's not leaving until next week."

J.R. stared at him. "Charlie?" he asked. "Haven't you heard? Old Charlie went down to Philadelphia with his mother and father on Saturday. His father had to be there early."

"I guess we've seen the end of Charlie," Gunther said. "It's up to you, Walter. You've got to get that arm in shape. I'll postpone the game for as long as I can."

The bell rang. Mrs. Mallory, the assistant principal, appeared out of nowhere to make sure everyone lined up. When the second bell rang, the fourth-grade class marched up to the second floor, where Mr. Dengle stood waiting for them in front of the classroom.

"What have you done now?" Mr. Dengle asked when he saw Walter.

Walter ducked his head. "A bush," he mumbled. "I mean a tree." He covered as much of the cast as he could with his right arm.

"Too bad, Walter," Mr. Dengle said. "Left-handed too, aren't you? Try to write with your right hand, if you can."

Walter nodded.

"Aren't you one of the ball players?" Mr. Dengle asked.

Walter nodded again.

Behind them J.R. spoke up. "We're just going to have to postpone the game again, Mr. Dengle. We can't play without old Walter."

Walter clutched at his arm, ducked past Mr. Dengle, and slid into his seat.

13

Walter collapsed into his seat behind Clyde Warner and began to shove his books into his desk. Casey was still watching him over her shoulder. He saw her eyes widen as he pushed his glasses up on his nose. Wrong hand.

He yanked it down again and banged the cast against the edge of his desk with a jarring wrench. A piece of the cast, as large as his thumbnail, flew through the air and landed on J.R.'s desk. Walter looked at it with horror.

It was a good thing J.R. was such a busybody. He was practically sitting in Richie Connors's lap at the desk next to his, talking about a ball game he had seen on television last night.

Walter looked around but no one seemed to be paying any attention to him. Mr. Dengle had put a list of spelling words on the board and most of the kids were copying them.

Walter leaned out into the aisle and grabbed the chip off J.R.'s desk. Then he sat back and felt the underpart of the cast gingerly. The spot where the piece had come off felt a little rough, but otherwise the cast seemed to be in pretty good shape.

Slowly, with his right hand, Walter pulled a piece of paper out of his desk, smoothed it a little, and picked up a pencil.

By this time J.R. had finished talking to Richie. He leaned over toward Walter. "Hey, Moles," he whispered loudly. "You should tell Mr. Dengle you can't write with that cast on your arm."

Walter looked at him irritably. "Will you quiet down a little," he said. J.R. was always getting him into trouble with Mr. Dengle because he whispered so much.

Walter bent over, pretending to get some paper out of his desk. He whispered back to J.R., "I've got to make it look as if I'm trying."

He straightened up and made a few faint, wiggly lines on his paper. Then he sighed as loud as he could and raised his right hand high in the air.

Mr. Dengle paid no attention. He was still writing on the board.

Walter waved his arm around and hissed a little to get Mr. Dengle's attention. Mr. Dengle put his chalk down and went to his desk without looking in Walter's direction.

"Hey," Walter called out finally. "Mr. Dengle."

Mr. Dengle looked up. "You're not supposed to call out, Walter," he said mildly. "You're supposed to raise your hand."

"I will the next time," Walter said. He made his face look as worried as he could. "I can't seem to write with my right hand."

Mr. Dengle looked at him for a moment without answering. Walter held up his paper. "I tried," he said, "but it doesn't seem to work."

Across the aisle and in front of him, Casey lowered her head. Walter could see she was trying hard not to laugh. He felt his own lips start to quiver, so he began to cough.

"You're really having a terrible time this morning," Mr. Dengle said.

Walter pounded his chest with his right hand. "Swallowed the wrong way. It's all right now." He lowered his eyes so he couldn't see Casey.

"Bring up the paper," Mr. Dengle said, "and let me take a closer look at it."

Reluctantly Walter heaved himself to his feet. He drew his cast in under his sleeve as much as he could and brought the paper to Mr. Dengle.

"Yes, I see," said Mr. Dengle. "Pretty shaky with that hand."

Walter nodded solemnly.

"I tell you what," Mr. Dengle said. "I'll excuse you from written work for the time being."

Walter ducked his head. "Gee, thanks, Mr. Dengle."

"All right. You may be seated now. But remember, you're not excused from studying."

Walter hurried back to his seat, making sure that he didn't look at Casey, who was curled over her seat with a Kleenex covering her mouth.

J.R. grinned at him. Under his breath, but loud enough for the rest of the class to hear, he said, "Wish there was something wrong with my arm."

"Don't feel bad," Gunther said. "There's something wrong with your head."

Everybody laughed, even J.R. But Mr. Dengle looked up from his desk, frowning. "That's enough, boys," he said. "It's time for us to get down to some composition work." He pursed his lips. "I'm going to do a paragraph at the board and I need some help." He glanced around at the class. "Since Walter can't write, he can come up here and tell me what to say."

Walter wished he could disappear. Slowly he stumbled up to the blackboard.

"All right, class," said Mr. Dengle. "I want you to watch us. In a few minutes you're going to do a paragraph. And I expect it to be as good as Walter's and mine." He flashed a brief smile at the class and turned to Walter, who was hunched over in front of the blackboard. "What do you want to write about, Walter?"

Walter shrugged.

Mr. Dengle pretended that Walter had spoken. "You say you're interested in baseball?"

Walter nodded.

"Right?" Mr. Dengle said.

"Right," Walter muttered.

"Well then, we'll write about that. Give me a first sentence."

Walter wet his lips. "Baseball is a good sport."

PATRICIA REILLY GIFF

"Good." Mr. Dengle wrote what Walter had said in round, white letters. He held his arms out. "You see how easy this is, class? Go ahead, Walter."

Walter couldn't think of one more thing to say. He cupped his right hand around the cast and stared at the floor. He had never really noticed it before. It had yellow and brown squares. Most of the yellow squares were covered with scuff marks from everyone's shoes.

"The fourth-grade team is going to play the fifth-grade team," Walter said faintly.

Mr. Dengle wrote the sentence on the board, then tossed the chalk up in the air a few times. "Can anyone help us?"

J.R. raised his hand. "A ball player needs a lot of coordination and practice."

"Absolutely right, Jonathan," Mr. Dengle told J.R. as he wrote the sentence on the board. "How about you, Gunther?"

"We're going to win the game—" Goony began.

"Yeah," J.R. shouted.

"—when Walter's arm is better," Goony continued. "The whole game depends on him."

Walter felt his face turn red. He looked out the window. He wished he were about a million miles away from here, somewhere . . .

"You're pretty important to the team," Mr. Dengle said, smiling. "We'll word it this way. As soon as my arm is better, I'll win the game for the team."

Mr. Dengle wrote the last sentence and made the period with a loud click of his chalk. "You may be seated, Walter," he said. "You did a fine job."

At his desk Mr. Dengle banged for attention. "Boys

86

"Go ahead, Walter," Mr. Dengle said.

and girls," he said, "before you begin your compositions, I want to talk to you about a couple of things."

The class looked up.

"Remember I promised you a class trip to the art museum?" Mr. Dengle paused and looked around. "You'll be excited to hear that the fourth and fifth graders are going this Friday."

As good as a day off—a three-day weekend, Walter told himself. Everybody started to talk at once.

"The purpose of this trip is culture," Mr. Dengle said. "It's not a goof-off day."

He held up his hand for order. "And now," he said when the class was quiet, "I want to talk to you about the science fair."

Walter leaned forward. If only he and Casey were chosen. They'd probably come up with a great project. In his imagination he could see a huge something on display, something that would probably revolutionize the whole world . . .

Mr. Dengle looked around. "Casey," he said, "you can be one of the representatives. I know you like science." He hesitated. "And . . ."

"Mr. Dengle," Casey called out. "How about Walter? He's the—"

Mr. Dengle shook his head and tapped his arm. "You forgot about Walter's cast, Casey. He couldn't possibly do a project with a broken arm."

Mr. Dengle looked around the class once more. "J.R.," he said, "you may represent the boys."

14

Friday morning Walter and Casey rushed out of the Best Food Delicatessen and into Gladys and Frank's Drug Store. According to Frank's big metal clock on the wall over the counter, they had about four minutes to get to school in time for the class trip.

There were two customers ahead of them. One was Mrs. Tutty. As Casey marched up to the counter, Walter ducked behind a big cardboard cutout of a bottle of hand lotion. He hoped Mrs. Tutty hadn't seen him.

It seemed to take her forever to decide between two different kinds of mouthwash.

"Walter," Casey called out. "Where did you go?"

Walter peered around the side of the cutout. "Here," he whispered. "Right over here."

Gladys leaned around Mrs. Tutty so she could see better. "Careful, Walter," she said. "Don't knock that thing over."

Mrs. Tutty turned around. She seemed to have forgotten about the other day. "What happened to your arm?" she asked.

She turned back to Gladys. "These children," she said before Walter had a chance to answer her, "always falling, breaking things, cutting themselves, getting into all kinds of trouble . . ." She paused and took a breath. "I think I'll take this bottle. It's a little cheaper. Besides, it's green. It will match the paper in my bathroom."

Frank looked over at Walter from behind the prescription counter and winked. Sheepishly Walter came out from behind the cutout and waited at the counter while Gladys made change for Mrs. Tutty and gave the next customer his newspaper.

"What can I do for you two today?" Gladys asked. She smiled at Walter and Casey. Walter noticed that she had very white teeth. He wondered if it was because she used a special kind of toothpaste that only drugstore people knew about, or if she tried all the different kinds that the store carried.

"We're going on a class trip today with the fourth and fifth graders," Casey told Gladys, "to the City Art Museum, and we're buying some snacks for the bus ride with the last of our money. We just got some potato chips next door—"

"Come on, Casey," Walter interrupted. "We're really

late and I have to drop this bag of cream puffs off at the Senior Citizens' Center. My grandmother made them for a cooking contest."

"Right, Walt," Casey said. "We need two packs of those orange slices, Gladys, and some malted milk balls, please."

Gladys nodded. "Give me your lunch bags and I'll pack everything right in."

Walter left the money on the counter and they raced out the door, yelling good-bye over their shoulders.

A few minutes later they stopped at the big red building where the senior citizens met, dropped off the cream puffs, then hurried down the block to arrive, panting, in front of the school.

The fourth- and fifth-grade lines were already there waiting for the doors of the special charter bus to open. Mr. Dengle frowned at Walter and Casey and looked at his watch. Then he clapped for attention. "All right, everybody," he said. "No nonsense now." He stood aside to let the fourth graders climb onto the bus.

Mrs. Butts, the fifth-grade teacher, rushed up to the bus door. "Wait a minute," she yelled. "Let Walter Moles in first. All we need is another accident."

Embarrassed, Walter went to the front of the line and took the first seat. Gunther Reed slid in next to him. "How are you doing, Walt?" he asked. "Have you tried to wiggle your fingers lately?"

"Not yet," Walter said. "I mean, I keep trying but nothing happens."

Gunther looked at Walter's fingers. "Give it a try, will you, Walt?"

Walter squeezed his eyes shut. "Trying," he said,

gritting his teeth. "Trying with all my strength." He shrugged. "Nothing."

On his way to the back of the bus, Rat Teeth leaned across Gunther and tapped Walter on the arm. "Hey. I hear you broke your arm just to get out of a baseball game."

"What kind of crazy talk is that?" J.R. said from the seat in back of them. "Walter's a hero. He won't talk about it but he probably saved someone's life."

Rat Teeth snorted.

"Don't you worry," J.R. went on, "old Moles'll be right out there in a couple of days, wiping up the floor with you guys." He nudged Walter. "Isn't that right, Moles?"

Walter took a deep breath. "I guess so. Right."

"Don't even answer him," Gunther said. "That Rat Teeth is an idiot, and J.R. is almost as bad."

Rat Teeth leaned over the seat. He stuck his face up close to Gunther's. "See that dirt out there. I ought to pile it in your mouth and plant a palm tree in the middle."

Gunther made a fist as Mrs. Butts poked her head into the bus. "What's this delay?" she scolded. "Move on, young man. Move on."

Rat Teeth glared at Gunther, then moved to the back of the bus.

"Don't pay any attention to him," Gunther said. "We'll show him when the cast comes off. We'll show Mr. Dengle too. That will be the end of Friday night homework."

Walter grunted. He looked out the window, trying to think of something to say. Finally he opened his

"I hear you broke your arm to get out of the game."

lunch. "Smells like lemon. My grandmother must have slipped some cream puffs in."

"All I can smell is that medicine on your cast," Gunther said.

Walter pulled his T-shirt sleeve down over his elbow and covered the cast with his right arm.

"Smells a little like flowers," Gunther said. "You know, those droopy-looking purple things . . ."

"Want a cream puff?" Walter broke in.

Gunther nodded.

"Take two."

Gunther reached into Walter's lunch. "Sure you don't mind?"

"Actually they're really not so good. Soggy."

In back of them J.R. stood up and leaned over the seat. The seat was so high Walter could only see J.R. from his mouth up. "Hey, you guys," J.R. said. "Did you see *Treasure in the Deep* on T.V. last night?"

"Do you have to start that again, J.R.?" Gunther asked. "Don't be such a pain."

J.R. ignored him. "Channel four. It was about this guy who was looking for treasure in an old ship. Turned out to be dope. Same guy who played in *Mystery Planet* last week. I can't remember his name. Well, anyway, it starts out when he was in the navy . . ."

Walter nodded a couple of times so that J.R. would think he was interested, then sat back and watched the houses. They seemed to be racing past the bus. He picked at a little piece of papier-mâché that was flaking off the end of the cast. He wondered how long he was going to have to wear the cast. He certainly wasn't spending much time practicing baseball. He

94

pictured himself wearing the cast into fifth and sixth grade, and even junior high, still trying to get ready for the game. He and Casey would have to keep making bigger casts as he grew out of them.

In the back of the bus everyone began to sing "Ninety-nine Bottles." Walter closed his eyes and half listened. Mrs. Butts told J.R. to sit down.

When they were down to seventeen bottles, the bus pulled up in front of the museum and they got off. Mrs. Butts led them inside while Mr. Dengle stayed in back of the line looking for stragglers.

"You may circulate," Mrs. Butts said. "Walk around on this floor and the next. But be back here"—she looked at her watch—"in one hour. Right in front of this painting."

Walter looked up at the painting. It was bigger than he was. The little sign underneath said "Lord Edklond." Walter noticed that the man in the painting had very pink cheeks and a red nose. It looked as if he had a terrible cold.

Casey came up to him. "That guy looks like a rabbit," she said.

Together they looked at the next painting. "Do you think this is Mrs. Edklond?" Walter asked. "She sure is fat."

"No, I think it's an angel. Could use some more clothes, if you ask me," Casey said.

Mrs. Butts drifted by. "It does inspire one, doesn't it," she breathed.

Casey followed her, giggling.

In back of him, J.R. pulled at Walter's shirt. "Come over here and look at this, Walt," he said.

Walter hesitated. He really wanted to go upstairs and see what was on the second floor.

J.R. pulled at him again. "Come on."

Walter shrugged and followed J.R. around the corner. J.R. cleared his throat. "There's something I wanted to talk to you about," he said.

The cast, Walter thought.

"About the science fair . . ."

Walter leaned back against the wall.

"I really feel bad that you weren't—"

"Listen, J.R.," Walter broke in. "I feel bad too. But it was my own fault. I mean . . ."

J.R. shook his head. "Yeah. If you hadn't been so brave, you'd have been the representative."

"Well . . ." Walter began uncomfortably.

"And the worst part of it is," J.R. said, "I thought I could use the pooter project. But Mr. Dengle says I did that so well, he thinks I'm capable of something even better."

Walter stood there thinking. "I'll help you," he said after a minute. "Next weekend."

"Gee, Walter," J.R. said. "That would be—" He broke off. "Hey. Look at that." He pointed to a white canvas that covered most of one wall. It was covered with names. On the wall beside it, attached to a metal cord, were a pen and a little card that said: GUESTS MAY ADD TO THIS DISPLAY. PLEASE SIGN YOUR NAME.

J.R. nudged him. "What does that remind you of?" he asked, grinning.

Walter pushed his glasses up higher on his nose and stared at the canvas. "I don't know," he said.

96

"Your cast," J.R. said. "Don't you see . . . all black and white like that."

"I guess you're right."

"And do you know what," J.R. continued. "We never signed yours. But don't worry, Walt. As soon as we get on the bus, I'll make sure everyone has a chance."

15

Caught. You're going to get caught. With every step Walter took toward the bus, the words danced a little jig in his head. He climbed up the steps and huddled into his seat, trying to hide as much of the cast as he could.

J.R. elbowed his way in front of Gunther and slid in next to Walter. "You don't mind, do you, Goony?" J.R. asked.

Gunther stopped dead in the aisle. "Get out of there, J.R. Walter and I were sitting together."

"Too bad for you," J.R. said. "I was here first."

In back of them Mr. Dengle started to yell. "Who's holding up the whole line? Is that you, Gunther? Get moving."

"You know, J.R., I'd like to use your head for a punching bag," Gunther said. He banged into the seat behind them.

J.R. knelt up and looked over the seat. "Hey, Gunther."

"Will you sit down," Mr. Dengle yelled as the bus began to move. "If I see anyone out of his seat before this trip is over, I'm really going to pile the homework on."

J.R. sat down again fast. He pushed his nose into the crack between his seat and Walter's.

"Hey, Goony," J.R. said. "Don't be mad. Come on. I wanted to tell you we forgot something."

"We didn't forget anything," Gunther answered. "Your mother did. She forgot to drown you when you were born."

"Very funny. What I wanted to tell you was that we forgot to sign Walter's cast." He turned back to Walter. "I've got a pen here somewhere," he said, rooting through his pocket.

"You're not going to sign my cast," Walter said.

J.R. hesitated. "Don't be silly. That's the best part of having a cast. All your friends getting a chance to—"

"No."

Gunther peered through the opening between the seats. "For once he's right, Walt. I'd like to—"

"Me first," J.R. said. "But I'll change seats with you after I'm finished." He fished a red pen out of his pocket and grabbed Walter's arm. "Hold still, Walt," he muttered. "I'm going to do my initials."

Desperately Walter tried to pull his arm away as J.R. dove for the cast.

In back of them Gunther yelled, "What's going on up there?" He peered through the crack between the seats.

J.R. gave one more tug and stabbed through the cast into Walter's arm.

"Yeow," Walter shouted. He looked down at the cast. A chunk in the middle had caved in, and as J.R. pulled his pen away, two cracks appeared at the edge of the hole and raced each other down the length of the cast.

J.R.'s mouth opened wide. "What . . . how . . ." he began.

In back of them Gunther started to shout. "I saw Walter wiggle his fingers. Walt, I think you've done it. You've moved your fingers."

Walter slapped his right hand over the cast. J.R. was still sputtering. "What kind of . . ."

"J.R." Gunther shouted. "Did Walter move his fingers?"

"I guess you could say that," J.R. said.

"What do you say, Walt? Can you get the cast off today, do you think?" Gunther asked.

Walter didn't answer.

J.R. stared at Walter's arm. "It's practically off now," he said.

Walter sighed.

"Hey, Rat Teeth," Gunther yelled. "We can play tomorrow. Walter's cast is coming off."

"Tomorrow's Saturday," Walter said faintly. "The

sixth and seventh graders will be using the schoolyard for their first big game."

"We'll have to play in the park, guys," J.R. called out. "How about one o'clock?"

"Who's running this game, anyway," Gunther said. "Make it one thirty, everybody."

"Stop that noise," Mr. Dengle said from somewhere behind them. He stamped up the aisle. "You two?" He glared first at J.R., then at Gunther. "Go sit in the back," he said, pointing at J.R.

Mr. Dengle stood there while J.R. threaded his way toward an empty seat next to Albert. Then he sat down next to Walter.

Walter risked a quick look at his cast. It was a mess. He grabbed his lunch bag and held it in front of the cast so Mr. Dengle couldn't see what had happened.

"What was that shouting about?" Mr. Dengle asked.

Walter cleared his throat. "My cast is coming off today so we're going to play tomorrow."

"Great, Walter, great. Who else will be playing?"

"Gunther, Clyde, Albert, Jimmy, Billy, J.R. . . ." Walter's voice trailed off. He wondered if J.R. was back there telling Albert that Walter's cast was nothing but . . .

". . . didn't know J.R. played ball," Mr. Dengle was saying.

"He wants to be a ball player, I think," Walter said.

"We can't all be great baseball players," Mr. Dengle said, smiling at Walter. "But J.R. can be proud of his own talent."

Walter searched his mind. The only talent J.R. had seemed to be making everybody crazy with all his talking.

"To be good at anything," Mr. Dengle went on, "you have to work at it. And J.R. Fiddle handed in one of the best science experiments I've seen in a long time. It was called a . . . a . . ." Mr. Dengle wrinkled his forehead.

"A pooter?"

Mr. Dengle nodded. "Exactly. A pooter." He leaned over Walter and looked out the bus window. "Back at school," he said, "just in time for dismissal."

Mr. Dengle stood up. "Good luck tomorrow," he said. "I'm going to make it a point to be at the park tomorrow afternoon so I can watch you guys mop up the place with the fifth-grade team." He swung into the aisle and went to the front of the bus.

As the doors opened, Walter stood up, hoping to get out of the bus before he had to talk to the rest of the kids. As he rushed down the aisle, Casey bounded up behind him. They nodded to Mr. Dengle as they climbed off the bus and headed across the schoolyard for home.

"Look," Walter said, holding out his arm.

Casey gasped.

"Let's get out of here," he said, "before the rest of the kids come along."

Together they raced out the side gate and cut across the lawn. Walter pulled off the cast as he ran. He stopped to dump the cast into the garbage can by the side of the house and cover it with some leaves and junk. Then he climbed the back steps into the house.

"I am the prize. I mean I won the prize."

His grandmother was in the kitchen. "Waltair," she said, "I've been waiting for you. Watching the clock."

Walter scratched his arm. "I have to go to the store or something?" he asked. The last thing he wanted was to run into one of the kids on the avenue.

"*Non.* I wanted to tell you. I am the prize. I mean I won the prize."

"Cream puffs," Walter said absently, still thinking about J.R.

"Not cream poofs. What a good boy you were to give up your lunch. You knew that was my best recipe all the time."

Walter blinked. "What?"

"Liver pâté and baby leeks on a loaf of homemade bread."

Walter shuddered. "Liver."

"It was mostly the bread," she said. "They loved my bread."

"That's good," Walter said and opened the laundry room door.

"We will celebrate," Mrs. Thorrien said. "I will make some bread and you can have your friends over tomorrow."

"There's a ball game tomorrow," Walter said slowly.

"After the game," she said. She got out the big blue mixing bowl. "Not the first prize," she mumbled to herself. "Not the second prize. But a prize." She nodded. "*Oui*, Walter, a prize."

Walter walked into the laundry room. He hoped his grandmother didn't make too much bread. He was sure that by tomorrow afternoon nobody would want to come home with him.

16

On Saturday Walter finished the last of his lunch. It
hadn't rained, he hadn't gotten sick, and his grandmother was rattling around in back of him baking
about a million loaves of bread.

He poked at his glasses. "I don't think anyone will be
coming here after the game," he said.

"Tush," Mrs. Thorrien said. "Make sure they do."
She looked at the clock. "Run along, Waltair. You
don't want to be late."

Slowly Walter pushed the chair back from the table
and went outside. Casey was in the driveway ahead of
him, bouncing a ball against the side of the house.

"Are you ready, champ?" she asked.

"Ready to run away or something," he said glumly.

"And my grandmother's inside waiting for the team to come home and celebrate."

"Look who's here," Casey said, pointing.

J.R. wobbled into sight on his bicycle, his bright green baseball hat pulled down over his eyes, balancing his bat on the handlebars. Braking with his feet, he slid to a stop in front of them. "Mind if I leave my bike against your house?"

"Go ahead," Walter said.

J.R. hopped off the bike and let it fall against the house. "How's the old wing, Moles?"

"All right, I guess," Walter said uncomfortably.

J.R. pushed his cap back. "Wheew! Was I worried! When I saw what I did to your cast, I thought I was going to be in some trouble." He shook his head solemnly. "I kept waiting for the phone to ring all night. I thought the doctor or your mother might—" He broke off and picked his bat up from the ground where it had fallen. "Reminds me of the movie *Dr. Goodbody Returns.* The hero was all bandaged up and . . ."

Casey looked at Walter as J.R. went on with his story. "Not blind," she mouthed. "Dumb."

"Come on, Moles," J.R. said after finishing his story. "It's game time."

"I think I'll just take a little walk down to the park myself," Casey said. "Watch the game for a while."

"I don't blame you," J.R. said. "With luck we may be finished with homework on weekends after this."

They turned in at the park gates a few minutes later and started up the bicycle path for the playing field.

Near the tables Walter saw Sonny leaning against a tree talking to another old man.

"Hey, kid," Sonny called over to Walter. "Going to play some baseball today?" He loped over to them and tweaked J.R.'s cap. "Looks like a major league hat."

J.R. nodded solemnly. "It's genuine all right. I got it at a Mets game last summer."

"Going to be a baseball player when you grow up, I guess."

J.R. flushed and shrugged. "I'm working at it," he said.

"Practice a lot?" Sonny asked.

J.R. nodded.

"Exercise?"

"Every day," J.R. said. "I'm studying up on all the players. Their averages, stuff like that."

"That's what it takes," Sonny said.

Suddenly it hit Walter. J.R. really was working at it. Every day. And the only reason J.R. wasn't the team shortstop was because of Walter. And Gunther's hot temper.

Sonny pulled a pipe out of his pocket. "Used to be a pretty good baseball player myself." He jerked his head toward Walter. "The kid here can tell you that." He put the pipe in his mouth and clamped his teeth around it. "Checkers player now," he said through gritted teeth. "Really good at that. Play every day."

"We have to go now," J.R. said. "We don't want to be late for the game."

Walter waved over his shoulder. He wished he were going with Sonny instead of going to the ball field. Scuffing his feet, he trailed along behind Casey and J.R.

Everybody was at the field already. Gunther was warming up on one side with Clyde, and the fifth graders were practicing on the other. Mr. Dengle sat in the bleachers drinking a bottle of ginger ale. Half the class sat with him. The fourth-grade team was wandering around waiting for Goony to tell them what to do.

Walter leaned against the end of the bleachers and looked at Casey.

"You know, Walt," she said in a low voice, "you're really home free. All you have to do is stand around in the shortstop's position, rubbing your arm like crazy." She climbed up on the bleachers. "Everyone will think you're still a hero, trying to play for the good of the fourth-grade team."

She was right. As usual. Walter craddled his left arm in his right and tried out a look of pain.

"Not bad," Casey said. "Not bad at all."

They sat down and watched J.R. do push-ups on the edge of the field. He was moving his lips, counting one and two and three and four. Every couple of minutes he had to stop and push his cap down over his forehead.

Poor J.R., Walter thought. It just wasn't fair. J.R. loved baseball the way Walter loved fooling around with science experiments. J.R. probably knew more about baseball than Carrots knew about catching mice. He drew in his breath sharply. J.R. must know that there weren't any left-handed shortstops.

For a moment he wondered why J.R. hadn't told the rest of the kids. Then he shook his head. J.R. was too good a friend.

He sat there a little longer, thinking. Finally he took a deep breath. He got up and walked slowly over to Gunther and Clyde.

"Hey," he yelled when he got close to them. "I've got to talk to you."

17

Gunther threw one last pitch to Clyde. "Your arm looks great, Walt," he said. "No more cast."

"Cast is in the garbage can."

"That's the way," Gunther said. "Ready to win the game?"

"Listen, Goony," Walter said, "I'm switching places with J.R."

"Did I hear right?" Gunther asked Clyde.

"I mean it," Walter said.

"I think you've gone crazy," Gunther said. "Sun's got to your head."

Walter shook his head. "You know what, Goony? I'm left-handed."

"So what?"

"I bet if you asked J.R., he could tell you that there's no such thing as a left-handed shortstop."

Gunther threw down his mitt. "What are you talking about?"

"Look, Gunther," Walter said slowly. "I'm no shortstop. I'm not even much of a ball player."

Behind them Rat Teeth began to yell. "Hey, Motor Mouths, do you want to hang around here all day or do you want to play some ball?"

Gunther glared at Walter. "Tell J.R. he can switch with you," he said as he picked up his mitt.

Walter felt his face redden. As he walked past J.R., he mumbled, "You're going to be shortstop today, J.R. I'll play left field."

J.R. followed him across the field. "How come, Walt? How come?"

Walter stopped walking. "How many left-handed shortstops are there in the major leagues, J.R.?"

J.R. pulled his hat down a little. "Well . . ."

"How many?"

J.R. leaned over toward Walter. "None, Walt."

"You knew all along that there is no such thing as a left-handed shortstop."

"Actually there was one, Willie Keeler," J.R. replied. "But that was in 1892." He fiddled with his cap. "Besides, Walt, I'd never tell anyone . . ."

Walter shook his head and sighed. "And about that cast . . ."

"I knew about that too. I saw it in the garage that day when it was still a lump of papier-mâché. I wasn't sure at first. You really did a terrific—"

"You knew . . ."

J.R. straightened his cap. "I hope you're not mad. I thought nothing would happen if I signed it. It looked pretty strong."

Walter stared at him incredulously. "You said you were up all night worrying."

J.R. shrugged. "Yeah. I didn't think you wanted me to know."

Walter shook his head slowly. "You're really something, J.R.," he said. "But if you want to win the game today, you'd better play shortstop. Besides, I told Gunther the truth about the shortstop business."

J.R. stood there for a minute. "All right, Moles," he said, "I'll do it. I can't let the team down."

Walter nodded and took off for left field. With a little luck none of the balls would come his way.

He watched Gunther wind up for the first pitch, then took a quick look at the bleachers. He gulped. Mr. Dengle was certainly going to find out that Walter wasn't the star of the team.

The first batter struck out. And so did the second. Rat Teeth was up third. He swatted the ball over second base. The fourth-grade right fielder scooped it up and threw it to first, but by that time Rat Teeth was sliding into second.

Walter watched him as he stood up, dusted off his pants, and began to yell directions to the next hitter. "Atta baby," he yelled. "Pitcher can't pitch. Fielders can't field." He danced back and forth at second base shouting at the top of his lungs.

Suddenly Rat Teeth was quiet. As Gunther wound up, he danced right off the base and tore for third.

"He's stealing," Walter screamed. "He's stealing."

But it was too late. By the time Gunther spun around and threw the ball to third, Rat Teeth was already there, safe. He began to yell at the hitter. "Send me home, baby. Thatta way."

The batter swung and connected with the ball. It bounced over the field, past J.R. and Walter. Rat Teeth and the batter went home.

From then on, the score seesawed back and forth. Walter was up four times. Each time he struck out without getting the bat off his shoulder.

By the last inning the score was even: seven up. Clyde led off with a single. By the time Walter was up again, there was one out and bases were loaded. Everyone was screaming.

Casey, leaning against the bleachers, looked at him sympathetically as he passed her on the way to the batter's box. This time he was determined to swing. Just let me connect, he pleaded with himself.

He missed the first two balls and hit the third. It dribbled halfheartedly to first, where Bobby Sanchez was waiting for it. Bobby caught it and tossed it to second for a double play.

Rat Teeth whooped with joy. "Extra innings," he shouted.

Gunther gathered everyone around him. "This is it, kids," he said. "We've got to keep them from scoring."

"They've made at least one home run every inning," J.R. said. "And Rat Teeth is up soon."

Walter stood on the edge of the group, thinking about Rat Teeth. He was always jumping up and down, screaming, stealing bases. "Hey," Walter said.

Gunther looked at him impatiently.

"A funny thing about Rat Teeth," Walter said. "I just realized. You can always tell when he's going to steal."

"What do you mean?" J.R. asked.

"Just before he steals, he stops yelling at everybody. I guess he's thinking about what he's going to do next."

"Listen to the expert," Gunther said.

J.R. nodded slowly, then clapped Walter on the back. "That's the old scientific mind working."

"A pair of experts," Gunther said.

Clyde looked at him. "Maybe you should shut up, Goony," he said. "Listen to somebody else for a change."

"Are we going to play today?" Rat Teeth screamed from the backstop.

Everybody raced back to his position. A few minutes later the first batter struck out. The second one did too. The third batter up was Rat Teeth. He smacked the ball and landed on first.

"We're gonna win this," Rat Teeth shouted. "Wait and see." He hopped up and down on base.

As the left-handed first baseman came up to bat, Walter looked toward J.R. He could see J.R. edging closer to second. He saw that Clyde was watching too.

Gunther wound up. Rat Teeth stopped yelling. Without hesitating, Gunther swiveled around and threw the ball to J.R. as hard as he could, as Rat Teeth tried to steal second.

Rat Teeth was out and the fourth graders were up again.

In the bleachers everyone was screaming. "Score," they yelled. "You gotta score."

Goony was up first and popped out. The crowd groaned. Then Walter watched as J.R. came up to bat next. J.R. was still the longest talker in the world, but somehow it didn't seem to matter anymore.

By this time, the fourth graders were stamping their feet on the bleachers shouting for a hit. J.R. bent over and rubbed his hands in the dirt. Then he scuffled his feet around. Walter could see he was nervous.

Suddenly everyone was still. J.R. tilted his hat, got into position, and swung.

Walter held his breath. The ball soared high out over the field and into the trees that edged the park.

The crowd screamed, and the fourth-grade team went wild as J.R. rounded the bases. They jumped up and down and pounded J.R. on the back. Goony was yelling louder than anyone. He socked Walter on the shoulder. "Terrific, Walt!" he screamed. "Terrific."

The fourth graders yelled, "Good game," to the fifth graders, then at the same moment, everyone remembered Mr. Dengle. The team flocked over to the bleachers.

"I know," Mr. Dengle said, standing up. "No homework on Fridays. Congratulations."

Casey jumped up on the bottom step of the bleachers. "Hey, everybody," she shouted. "Walter's grandmother is having a celebration at Walt's house."

Everyone turned toward Walter. He poked at his glasses. "If you want to come," he said. "Everyone's invited."

"Race everyone there," Gunther yelled and took off across the field with most of the fourth graders following him. J.R. stayed behind, near Walter.

Walter looked up. "You want to come, Mr. Dengle?" he asked faintly. "There's something I want to talk to you about."

Mr. Dengle jumped off the bleachers. "Is it about the game?"

Walter nodded.

"And pooters," J.R. chimed in.

"And confidential experiments?" Mr. Dengle asked. "Made out of papier-mâché?"

"How . . ." Walter began. He took a deep breath. "I'm the ecologist, Mr. Dengle," he began.

J.R. straightened his hat.

"And he's the ball player," Mr. Dengle and Walter said together.

From the checkers tables Casey shouted back, "Are you coming?"

"How about some homemade bread, Mr. Dengle?"

Mr. Dengle grinned. "Why not?" he said. "Let's go."

About the Author

Patricia Reilly Giff

was born in Brooklyn, New York. She holds degrees from Marymount College and Saint John's University. A reading consultant, she has published four books, including *Fourth-Grade Celebrity* and *The Girl Who Knew It All*.

Mrs. Giff lives in Elmont and Harvard, New York, with her husband and three children.